Scotch Mist

Dottie Manderson mysteries book 3: a novella

Caron Allan

Scotch Mist: Dottie Manderson mysteries book 3: a novella

ISBN: 9781717477934

SCOTCH MIST

DOTTIE MANDERSON MYSTERIES

BOOK 3: A NOVELLA

.

With grateful thanks to my family

Day One: Tuesday

Anna McHugh glared through the prison bars at the sprawling body. When the figure did not immediately acknowledge her presence, she aimed a kick through the bars at the foot hanging off the end of the narrow cot.

'Hey, idiot! I haven't got all day to wait around for you, so let's get going.'

The figure on the cot stretched and yawned in a leisurely manner, as if awaking from a deep refreshing sleep. He got to his feet and gave her what he clearly believed was a cheeky smile, but she glared at him again and turned on her heels.

'If you're no' in the street in one minute, you'll have to walk back.' She returned to the waiting area at the front of the police station, saying to the officer behind the desk, 'He's ready to leave now, if that's all right.'

The police officer gave her a grin as he turned to

fetch the keys out of a cupboard behind him. 'Just out the three days, isn't it? I know you said he was at home with you all night. But we all know it was him that took that deer from Barr Hall. And the laird is a very good friend of the procurator. So maybe try and keep your man home at night, m'dear, if you don't want him to go straight back to prison. Next time it could be for a wee bit longer.'

She watched Constable Forbes go through to unlock the cell door. 'He's no my man,' she said softly.

Her man was at home, behind the bar of his public house, and he would be ready with his belt when he heard she'd given William Hardy an alibi for the previous night. Her heart felt heavy. She dreaded going home. But what else could she do? She couldn't let Will go back to jail for the one crime he hadn't committed. She went out into the sunshine to the little car she'd borrowed from the pub.

It seemed everything she did for Will got her into trouble. How could he have given up her name like that, even to get himself out of a tight spot? Surely he knew by now the price she would pay for that? Her mind whispered that her mother would have said a true gentleman never betrayed a lady's confidence. But William Hardy was no gentleman, and she doubted he would say she was a lady, either. Why did she let him do this to her? If she could only get him out of her life—and her heart—perhaps her husband wouldn't find so much fault in her. Which would mean far fewer bruises.

She sat behind the wheel, waiting. And waiting. She told herself she'd just give him another minute, then it became two more, and then another five. Finally after almost fifteen minutes the man appeared, swaggering as he came, proud as punch of his exploits. Along the street someone cheered, and Will raised his fist in a gesture of triumph. Anna sighed. How was another night in the cells anything to be proud of?

The same day, London.

Mrs Carmichael's funeral was every bit as awful as Dottie had feared.

Mrs Carmichael had no relations that Dottie was aware of. The church was packed with the dead woman's few close friends and a crowd of former customers, all dressed to the nines in the most costly of Mrs Carmichael's creations they had in their possession, vying to outdo one another in glamour. A sea of black-dyed ostrich-plumed hats had blocked the entire front of the little church from Dottie's view. The cloying stench of too many hot-house flowers threatened to overwhelm the senses. Two ladies had prolonged sneezing fits due to the pollen and had to be led outside to wait in the entryway.

The rain—having held off for several grey days— descended now in torrents, reducing the graveyard to little more than a bog, which was why the service had to be held inside. Dottie never did actually catch sight of the coffin, even though, due to the size of the lady reposing inside it, she somewhat irreverently assumed it to be a large one.

Mrs Carmichael had been horribly murdered just a few weeks earlier, and her fashion warehouse was silent, in a kind of limbo, with no business being done. Like the other mannequins, Dottie had no idea what was going to happen either to her job or the warehouse itself, or to the half-planned spring-summer 1935 collection. The place just wouldn't be the same without the large, formidable woman shouting orders in her strident East London accent, scattering the girls here and there. Dottie just couldn't picture a future for the warehouse. Her late employer had spent her whole life building the business up single-handedly, and now what was to become of it?

It was a terrible occurrence. Dottie couldn't bear to think about Mrs Carmichael being pushed down the stairs of her own home in the middle of the night. In recent months Dottie had known of several people who had died unpleasantly. But the death of Mrs Carmichael, who had been a friend as well as an employer, had hit her hard and she found herself continually on the verge of tears, not wanting to think about it, yet finding it was all she could think about.

The only bright note in an otherwise miserable day was when Police Inspector William Hardy entered the church. She caught his eye immediately and her heart sang when he smiled and came to sit beside her.

The service began. The large congregation, for once, did justice to the demands of funeral hymn-singing, and Dottie's clear contralto blended well with Hardy's robust baritone. For several minutes she was so thoroughly immersed in the pleasure of singing with him that she completely forgot the sad occasion.

At the end of the service, it was still too wet for either coffin or congregation to proceed into the graveyard, and so after hanging about for half an hour, conversing in muted tones, the mourners dispersed, dashing outside under large umbrellas to step thankfully into cars. Dottie's parents, along with her sister and brother-in-law, began to make their way to their own vehicles. Dottie held back, wanting to spend a few more minutes with William. But she was disappointed.

He walked with her as far as the church door, then looking about and seeing no one watching, he dropped a self-conscious kiss on her cheek and said, 'Sorry, I'm afraid I must dash. I have an appointment I mustn't miss. May I telephone you?'

'Of course you may, but...'

And he was gone, waving regretfully over his shoulder. Damn the man, Dottie thought furiously, with scant regard for the hallowed place in which she was standing. Every time she thought she'd finally got a few minutes with him, he ran off! At least this time he had kissed her. In a manner of speaking.

An hour later, at the premises of Bell, Bray and Mower, Solicitors, Dottie was shown into the office of Mr Bray, the senior partner. As she followed the bald young man who was Mr Bray's secretary, she collided with a tall, lean figure. Glancing up on hearing someone say her name, she saw William Hardy standing there.

She felt flustered at coming across him so unexpectedly. Was this the appointment he had mentioned? Why was he here? He appeared equally uncomfortable. But she had only time to say, 'William! What on earth...?' before she was chivvied into the room he had just left, and was more or less herded into a leather armchair. The door closed as William glanced back through the gap of the closing door and gave her an apologetic shrug.

Mr Bray, introducing himself, wasted no time in embarking on a long speech about his role as Mrs Muriel Carmichael's legal representative as it related to her last will and testament.

Of course, thought Dottie, her mind still fixed on

William Hardy. He's probably had to come here on a police matter—his work was all about the miniscule detail of legal proceedings. No doubt he was here in an official capacity, looking into something or other to do with Mrs Carmichael's murder.

She was mulling these thoughts over, pleased with the idea that it was 'only' work that kept William from her side, when it gradually dawned on her that the other occupant of the room had fallen silent. Mr Bray had talked at length and then stopped, and she had no idea what he had said.

She gazed at him with her lovely hazel eyes. Mr Bray, a mousy, timid bachelor in his mid-fifties, was very fond of dark-haired girls with lovely hazel eyes. It was fortunate he was, because he now had to say everything again. Normally Mr Bray was not a patient man, but with her eyes upon him now, he happily told her the good news all over again.

'Muriel Carmichael not only thought of you as an employee but also as a friend. As such, and in view of your dedication, hard work and commitment to your position in her warehouse, coupled with Mrs Carmichael's lack of close family, I am instructed to hand over the entirety of Mrs Carmichael's assets to you, with three notable exceptions.'

Dottie couldn't begin to understand what Mr Bray was telling her. Assets? What assets? What could he mean?

'There is, however, one requirement that must be fulfilled before those assets can actually become yours. I hope that you will not find the demand placed on you too onerous.' He gazed upon her pleasing features. He knew she worked as a mannequin in Mrs Carmichael's fashion warehouse, and certainly he could see why she was so valued by his client. He hoped—fervently—that she was not grasping. She was lovely, to be sure, but he had met ladies before who were lovely on the outside only. Sometimes, outer beauty, brittle and hard as a mask, concealed the inner ugliness of a cold, grasping heart. The love of money...

'A requirement?' Dottie repeated. 'And assets? What assets?'

'Everything Mrs Carmichael owned is now yours...'

'Every...?'

'...apart from three properties she has disposed of elsewhere, and her vehicles.'

Dottie was staring at him without comprehension. Mr Bray, being an old-fashioned sort of chap, was hopeful that Dottie was, as befitted a true lady, in need of guidance in these complex affairs.

'Mrs Carmichael left the business to me! The warehouse, everything!' Dottie exclaimed to her sister, Flora, before she even entered the house. Greeley, Flora's butler, ushered her into the hall with an expression of undisguised interest.

Flora was every bit as astonished as Dottie had hoped, and never one to be concerned about keeping private things private from her own staff, she immediately began to cross-examine Dottie about it. 'The whole business? The warehouse and the designs?'

'Everything!' Dottie said. She was dizzy with trying to take it all in. 'Not the house in France—can you believe she had a colossal fortune? She even had a house in France! That's to go to her maid, Pamphlett. And the London house she lived in, she's left that to someone else too. I don't know who. I know it's none of my business, but all the same, I should have liked to know. And there's a little cottage somewhere, I forget where, down on the south coast, that's gone to someone else again. And then it turns out she had several cars, they're garaged in a mews not far from her house, and are to go to yet another person. It really is very frustrating not knowing who these people are, not that I care a fig about cars, though I do want George to teach me to drive... Where was I?' She paused for breath. Flora—and Greeley—were still staring at her. 'Oh yes, everything else—savings, stocks and shares, investments, and her personal items: jewellery, the furniture at the warehouse, and then there's the warehouse itself, the designs, all the stock, the orders, it's all been left to me, lock stock and barrel! A small apartment in Covent Garden. Another little house somewhere, I can't remember where. It's all so—I don't know...'

'Exciting?' suggested Flora.

'Wonderful?' suggested Greeley.

A light went out in Dottie eyes. She leaned forward and in a sober voice, she said, 'It's worth almost a million pounds. It's all too much. How can one person own so much? It's jolly scary actually. It seems like such a huge responsibility.' She slumped down in an armchair. 'I can't seem to take it all in.' She looked up at Greeley, hovering in the doorway, her coat and hat still in his hands. 'Could I please have a cup of tea, Mr Greeley?'

Greeley collected himself. He had been drinking in every word. 'Oh yes, of course, Miss Dottie.' And he hurried away, eager to share the latest news with his wife, who was Flora and George's cook, and the maid Cissie.

Below stairs, whilst waiting for the kettle to boil, they toasted Dottie's good fortune, Greeley adding solemnly that she deserved it, she'd been so very fond of the old woman.

In the drawing room, Flora and Dottie had resumed their interminable knitting.

'I hope you don't have another baby for at least five years,' Dottie grumbled. 'I can't even bear the sight of a ball of wool now. It will take me at least five years to recover from all this knitting. Why you didn't just buy everything, I'll never know.'

At seven months' pregnant, Flora looked—and felt—very large. She also felt exhausted. 'I wanted nice things, proper things, made specially for my baby, things that mean something. Anyway, just nine more weeks or so... although babies don't always arrive on time. I do hope it's not too late, I'd hate to have problems. I don't know which is worse, not sleeping now because I can't get comfortable, or not sleeping after the baby arrives due to getting up at all hours of the night.'

'You won't be getting up at all hours, it'll be the poor nurse you and George employ. Anyway, it'll be nice to be able to see your feet again,' Dottie pointed out helpfully. Flora threw a ball of wool at her.

'So what's next? Do you just go to the warehouse tomorrow and tell everyone that you're now in charge?'

Dottie wrinkled her nose. 'No. I've got to do an errand first. Quite a big one. To earn my inheritance. If I don't do it, I can't have the money, so of course I said I would do it immediately. I've got to find someone for Mrs Carmichael, or rather for Mr Bray.'

'Oh?' Flora said. 'Who?'

'Her son.'

'Her...? I didn't know she'd ever been married. I thought that Mrs Carmichael thing was just a blind?'

'It was. She wasn't.'

'Oh.' They looked at each other.

'Yes, it's exactly what you think. Some chap got her into trouble when she was a young woman then left her in the lurch. She had to give the baby up for adoption. It's bad enough these days when a girl gets into trouble. In those days, what, thirty or so years ago, it must have been even worse.'

'I can imagine.'

'So I've got to go to Scotland and see this person, and let them know that she was their mother and that she has now passed away, and I've got to get them to contact the solicitor. And when they do that, I will get my inheritance. And I'm assuming they will get theirs.'

'Scotland!'

'Yes, I'm to go to a little place near Edinburgh, but on the coast. Apparently the solicitor Mr Bray has been looking for Mrs Carmichael's baby and that's where he's tracked him to. It's a boy. Well. Or rather, a man, I suppose. Anyway I haven't actually got to track the person down, just wait to find out their address then go and tell them the news.'

'Why doesn't this Mr Bray go himself, or get a policeman to call on the fellow? Or write? Doesn't Mr Bray know that you can actually just send letters to people? I don't see why you should drag yourself all the way up to Scotland.'

'Well Mr Bray's a terribly busy man, and it's part of me getting the inheritance. Mrs Carmichael said she wanted me to do it. So...' She shrugged again. 'Mr Bray's rather a dear old pet. I bet he's not married, he's probably just got a faithful old dog for a companion. He seems to feel that it's a situation requiring a certain feminine delicacy. It's all a bit cloak-and-dagger. Perhaps the baby's terribly respectable now and doesn't want anyone to know about his illegitimacy? People can be unforgiving of something like that. He says the estate will pay my expenses, but warns me it's only a little village and won't have all the usual comforts. Anyway, when I arrive at the hotel, I'm to meet with someone who will tell me how to find this fellow. And this is all a huge secret. I'm not allowed to tell anyone, or... What? Why are you looking at me like that?'

'A secret, Dottie! Darling, you've just told me everything!'

'Well, obviously! I'm hardly going to whizz off to Scotland without a word to anyone.'

Flora shook her head and smiled to herself. 'It's quite exciting. Just like a detective story. I'd love to come with you, but George—and Mother—would have forty fits at the idea of a woman in my condition going all the way to Scotland.' She sighed. 'I have absolutely no fun at the moment. I'm not even twenty-four until August, but I'm just a fat old woman, my youth is behind me.'

'True,' said Dottie, not caring a jot. 'But once the baby's arrived, you'll soon be back to form, dancing, shopping, all the usual things. It's not going to last forever.'

'It feels like forever,' Flora complained. 'I suppose you've got to go up on the train?'

'How else does one get to Scotland? Yes, I'm going up on the Flying Scotsman. I've got a seat reserved for the day after tomorrow. So I need to get home and tell Mother, and give her a chance to rant and rave, and then tomorrow I can pack and get ready. Mr Bray has taken care of everything. He's made me a reservation at a hotel in a little place called Lower Bar, on the east coast. It's all happening so quickly. It's so exciting!'

'Mother will never let you go all that way on your

own.'

'She will, because if I don't go, I shan't get the inheritance. And she won't want that to go to some cat's home.'

In his pocket was the envelope containing the train ticket, the confirmation of his hotel reservation, and a large amount of money. The envelope was a full and large one, the corners of it poked out and spiked his wrist. But he didn't care, he felt excited. He was to go to Scotland, and he was to use his detective skills to track down a missing heir. It was all irresistibly romantic, like something from a book. No one was to know where he was going apart from his immediate superiors at work, and he was allowed one phone call to his sister to let her know he would be away.

Eleanor was still staying with their uncle and aunt in Matlock, Derbyshire. She had been there since the death of their mother two, almost three months, earlier, and her conversation, when he made the expensive call to her once a week, was mostly a recital of all her socialising with a young man of whom she was increasingly enamoured. His aunt had warned him several times to expect an announcement, and he had made sure of both his own and his sister's financial situation, in case of just such an occurrence.

That was partly what this trip was about. He hadn't mentioned it to the chief superintendent, but Mr Bray had given him a cash payment of £250 in addition to his expenses, and had promised him a further £250 on successful completion of the task he had been set. Inspector William Hardy, of the Metropolitan police force, was not in a position to turn down £500 in cash when he had a younger brother at public school and a sister on the verge of marriage.

But.

All this meant he would not be able to see Dottie Manderson. To make matters worse, because he had been sworn to secrecy, he couldn't even let her know he was going to be away. Not for the first time, it seemed he had to put his own wants and needs on hold in order to do something for someone else. When, he wondered, would he finally be the one at leisure to do the courting, the proposing, the leading to the altar?

He reached the lodging house where he had recently taken a room to save money on living expenses, and paused to unlock the front door. He comforted himself that it was likely he would only be away for a week. In a week, or less if he was fortunate, he would have completed this task for Mr Bray, and would have plenty of time to talk to Dottie, to take her for dinner, and even—he was daydreaming now—ask her to marry him.

It took him five minutes to pack: he didn't have a large wardrobe of suits and shirts. He was to go up the next morning on the Flying Scotsman, drive a rented car from Edinburgh to the small coastal village of Lower Bar, and stay at the hotel there. He would meet with someone to gain information. Then he would follow up that information to find this missing heir. Then, and only then, could he gain the written confirmation he needed, so he could return to London to claim the remaining money. Even if he wasn't successful—and he hoped he would be, he'd promised himself he would do his utmost to succeed—he would still have an extra £250 in his pocket and have had a trip to Scotland and a short holiday in a hotel. He felt quite excited about the whole thing. Perhaps adventure was too strong a word, but he felt as though something significant was going to happen.

Mr Bray went home to his cat, and his sister, at the end of a long day at the office.

He waited for his sister to prepare and serve his dinner. The cat, who had already eaten, came to sit on his lap in front of the fire. In the Bray household, even though it was the beginning of May, a fire was still lit in the small sitting room at the back of the house, overlooking the garden. The evenings were still inclined to be a little chilly and Mr Bray, wealthy enough to please himself, didn't care to be chilly. So he and the little black cat sat in front of the fire and thought about life.

He drank a small glass of sherry. The cat purred as he stroked her, and Mr Bray thought about his day at the office. Mrs Carmichael's will was rather more straightforward than he had led either Inspector Hardy or Miss Manderson to believe. But he felt that having placed his own demands on the two young people, he was fulfilling the spirit of her will, in addition to its actual provisions.

He thought back to the long discussion he had had with the departed lady some months earlier, and remembered her disclosures about her early life and Mr Hardy's father's role in that: her confession of the long-lost romance, and the cherished baby she'd had to give up. She had wanted to know that her child was provided for and secure. She had wanted an end to secrets and deception.

Well here was a way to do that, Mr Bray thought.

Mrs Carmichael had talked with animation and affection of the young mannequin who was more than a mere employee to her, and whom she knew to be enamoured of the younger Mr Hardy.

Mr Bray smiled. He was confident that everything would go just as he had planned. He thought it was all so very romantic, and Mr Bray, though a middle-aged bachelor, was very keen on romance. He believed Mrs Carmichael, less romantic but very fond of the people involved, would have approved. It all seemed very fitting. Because if her death had proved anything, he reflected, it was that life was short, and often brutal. Death always came a little sooner than expected, so it was essential that one made the most of every opportunity that came one's way, for who knew if another would ever come along? He knew from his own experience that romantic opportunities came only rarely.

When his sister called him to the dinner table, she said, 'So, did it all go as you planned?'

'Oh yes,' he said. 'It went perfectly.'

'I'm surprised they just accepted it. Mrs Carmichael never put it in her will they had to find her son, did she?'

'No, but if she'd had time to think about the problem, I'm sure she would have had the same idea as myself. And the son in Scotland has got to be told.'

'You could have simply written to the young fellow. Or telephoned.'

'I wanted the other son to meet him. They should meet, get to know one another, that's only right. But the inspector wouldn't have gone if I'd simply told him the truth. This way he'll find out the truth for himself, and hopefully be forced to accept the situation. Who knows, the two men could become friends. After all they share a name.'

'Two names, surely?' His sister shook her head in disapproval. 'Bad enough to have a son out of wedlock, but then a year or so later, to give your legitimate son the same name... What was the father's name again?'

'Major Garfield Hardy.'

'Well I think it was very poor of him. What was wrong with the man? Had he no sense of responsibility? No sense of propriety? And him a Major in the British Army. I feel I should have disliked him very much.'

Mr Bray nodded and sighed. 'It's an odd situation. And clearly he was not all that he could have been. But his son—his legitimate son, I mean, seems to be made of stronger stuff. And hopefully—oh I do so hope—the two young men will meet, and eventually, reconcile their feelings. It's only fair that the Scottish half-brother should be provided for. If my information is anything to go by, his need is desperate.

'And Miss Manderson?'

'Miss Dottie? Well, she also has to prove her mettle. In addition to which, she is very charming. I believe the news will be best delivered in person by her. It will soften the blow considerably, having her there. For both men. And throwing her and the inspector together in this way... well I can only hope nature will take its course. Yes, all in all, I have every hope of a happy outcome for everyone involved.'

'Well we shall soon see.' His sister smiled and shook her head indulgently as she bustled back to the kitchen. He was as fond as an old woman.

*

Day Two: Wednesday

William Hardy sat on the train. The countryside was rushing by, now and then in a smoky, steamy veil as the engine worked its way up an incline. London was already miles behind him. The train was only half-full, possibly because it was midweek, and apart from the sound of the train itself, there was no other noise to distract him in his corner seat.

He leaned back against the padded headrest, resisting the urge to close his eyes, afraid the movement of the train would lull him to sleep, because he needed to think. His financial problems were proving difficult to resolve. This errand for Mr Bray couldn't have come at a better time. He hadn't realised just how badly his mother's portfolio had suffered in recent years, and now she had died, he was finding all sorts of little discrepancies she had kept to herself. If only his brother's school would give him more time to pay the arrears on the fees...

Outside a bright sun shone down on a varying

view of countryside and towns, farms and factories. In a little while, lunch would be served in the sumptuous dining car. That evening, he would be eating dinner at a hotel in Edinburgh before driving the hired car to Lower Bar where he would stay the first two nights, and as many subsequent nights as it took to accomplish Mr Bray's aim.

He had been to Edinburgh twice before. One day he hoped to go right up to the northernmost point of the country. One day. He had travelled all over the south and the west of the United Kingdom as a boy, and all over the east too. In the days before the money was gone, there had been family holidays, trips and outings, visits to his mother's family in Derbyshire, and his father's in Kent.

And he'd been to parts of Europe: to France and Belgium, to see where his father had been as a soldier in the Great War, to places still showing the scars and dereliction of those terrible days. As a student, with friends he'd travelled to Egypt, and even to New York and Washington DC in America, on an ocean liner where he'd stayed out on deck all day every day, even in the worst weather, captivated by the ever-changing face of the sea, never tiring of the undulating waves.

Being on a train was a little like being on a ship, he thought, as the carriage swayed on a long slow bend...

'Now taking the second sitting for lunch, sir,' the guard said, waking Hardy from a dream of walking by the ocean, Dottie at his side. He was surprised to see it was still daylight outside; he felt as though he had slept for hours. He thanked the guard, and rousing himself, slowly shaking off the dream, he got to his feet and made his way unsteadily to the dining car.

They arrived slightly ahead of schedule. He wished he could have stayed the night in Edinburgh. He would have liked to take the opportunity for a walk around the city, perhaps even a look at the castle brooding up on the hill above the streets. If only he'd thought to mention it to Mr Bray... but of course, he wasn't actually on holiday, he reminded himself for the umpteenth time, he was working, on a mission, and therefore not at leisure to please himself.

He left the platform, giving up his ticket at the barrier and crossing the concourse to exit the grand Victorian building. He made his way, guided by Mr Bray's written instructions, to the hotel where he ate his dinner in the charming dining room, then as soon as he had finished his coffee, he went along to the garage where he was to collect his rented car. He wondered if he should pause at a newsagent's to buy a map, but found the garage had provided one. In less than ten minutes, he was edging the unfamiliar vehicle out into the busy evening streets and heading for the coast.

By half past nine that evening he was sitting on the bed in his room, and deciding that it would have to do. The room was small, gloomy, and in need of a fresh coat of paint, but the bed seemed comfortable. There was a window looking out on the front of the hotel. A small wardrobe that wobbled slightly when he opened the door that stuck a little. A tallboy for his clothes, should he bother unpacking. There was a connecting door leading to the next room which he supposed would be useful for family groups.

The 'hotel' was in fact merely an inn, and a small one at that, named rather disappointingly, The Thistle. It was one of two public houses in the village, which also boasted: a church with a surprisingly large graveyard, a sprawling patch of cottages, a joint post office and general store, a small shop selling knitting wools, ribbons and such like, and not much else. It was picturesque in the same style as many other Scottish villages, with a typical stone bridge over a typical narrow brown river, and though nice enough in its own way, it was hardly the kind to be featured on the lid of a chocolate box. He had seen prettier places on his drive from Edinburgh that evening.

He had a day and a half until his meeting with the mysterious person Mr Bray had arranged for him to see. Plenty of time for him to get a feel for the area. He went down to the bar to see about the arrangements for meals.

The Thistle had few other guests. It appeared to possess only five guest rooms, to judge by the keys hanging behind the bar which doubled as desk and reception area. Only two keys were absent, presumably his own and that of the stout elderly lady who sat beside the fire, an aged, obese Pekinese sprawled on her lap. The dog yapped loudly and excitedly as Hardy walked by, the sound echoing around the wooden panels and stone floor. The electric lightbulb overhead showed the dust and fur drifting from the dog down towards the ground, stirred up by the vigorously wagging topknot of a tail. The woman tapped impatiently on the stone floor with a walking stick. She peered closely at Hardy when he bid her good evening, curled her lip and turned away without responding, so he felt it was unlikely they would become friends.

Just as he was turning away, a man hurried into the bar, almost bumping into Hardy.

'Beg pardon, sir,' he said hastily, without really looking. He leaned over the bar to call out towards the back room. 'Hey, Nelson! Has the man from London arrived yet?'

'That's him you almost killed in your rush, Gregg, man.' The barman, wiping a glass with a white cotton cloth, indicated Hardy with a poke of his head. The new chap, Mr Gregg, whirled round, eyeing Hardy in relief.

'What, you're the policeman?' As if he couldn't believe his luck.

Hardy, with some surprise, admitted he was a policeman, and that he had just arrived from London. He reached for his warrant card to show them.

Gregg and Nelson leaned in to stare open-mouthed at it. They exchanged a look. 'That's interesting,' said Nelson to Gregg.

'Isn't it just?' Gregg responded, though neither of them saw fit to enlighten Hardy. 'Oh, sorry sir, but I've been sent down to collect you. You're to come straight away. The laird doesn't like to be kept waiting.'

Hardy frowned. 'Oh well, of course, though I'm not...'

'As quickly as you can, sir, if you don't mind. We can talk as we go, if there's anything you need to ask me.'

'What exactly is the problem?' Mr Bray hadn't said anything about meeting with a laird, but perhaps the laird was his contact? He hurried after the man. They were out of the door now, and into the clear golden twilight of the spring evening. A chill wind blew in off the sea, along the length of the street, and out across the moors to the north, but the glorious sky made up for the low temperature.

'Best I leave it to the laird to tell you all about it, sir. Up you go.' He assisted Hardy to mount up into a small horse-drawn cart, and almost immediately they set off. After five minutes, they'd scarcely covered any ground, and the picturesque mode of transport frustrated Hardy with its lack of speed.

'If I'd known,' he remarked, 'we could have used my car.'

Gregg immediately pulled up the horse to a standstill. 'A motor car, sir?' Clearly, he couldn't believe it. His voice actually trembled with excitement. 'Will we go back and get it? I can collect the horse later. I'll give her a nosebag whilst we're gone, if you like.'

The hope in his voice was unmissable. Obviously few cars came through the village, though Hardy would have expected someone as high-sounding as a laird would have his own motor, perhaps even a whole garage of them. Hardy weighed the options and decided that even with the time it took them to turn the cart and go back to the village, it could hardly be as slow as going the whole distance by horse and cart.

'Yes,' he said. 'We will.'

Gregg, carried away by his excitement, turned the cart at such a speed that it almost overturned, and he drove back into the village considerably faster than they had come out of it. In less than three minutes they had returned, disposed of the horse and were already in Hardy's rented vehicle and on their way once more.

Hardy was both amused and irritated by Gregg's round-eyed wonder and incessant questions. Ten minutes later they pulled off the road and onto the long sweep of a gravel drive that curved uphill to a large elegant house. A small plaque on the wall beside the wrought iron gates proclaimed their arrival at Barr Hall. As they came to a halt behind the house, Hardy found himself agreeing to let Gregg 'have a go' on the morrow.

It was a relief to park the car, get out and stretch. It had already been a very long day, what with the trip up from London. He was feeling drowsy, and his eyes were playing tricks on him. He was convinced he saw his own reflection peering at him through the trees a few yards beyond one of the outhouses. He stumbled, and his brain seemed to freeze for moment. Where was he, behind the tree, or here looking back at it? He shook himself, and pushed the odd fancy away. He just needed a good night's sleep.

Gregg took Hardy in at the back door and introduced him to the butler, a Mr Roberts, who brought Hardy along the hallway to knock on the door of what proved to be the study.

'Wait here,' the butler told Hardy.

An imperious male voice bid them, 'Come,' and Roberts went in. Hardy made out a murmur of conversation, then Roberts reappeared and beckoned him into the room.

Hardy entered the study to see a tall man dressed in evening attire, waiting on the far side of a bearskin rug beside the fire across the vast expanse of the room. The man made no attempt to close the space between them either by stretching out a welcoming hand, or offering a simple greeting. He remained where he was, sipping brandy from a snifter, his free hand hooked negligently into a pocket. He watched Hardy's approach as if looking down a very long nose.

When Hardy was just a few feet from him, the man finally said, 'Ah, Inspector Hardy, is it? I've been expecting you.'

Irritated both by the supercilious manner and the ridiculous waste of life that had provided the bearskin, Hardy carefully stepped around the dead animal's head to hold out his hand to the gentleman. The man stared at his hand but ignored it. Hardy's irritation grew. Usually patient and cautious, on this occasion he allowed his feelings to goad him into saying, 'I hardly see how you could be expecting me, sir, since I didn't know myself I was going to be here this evening. I simply happened to be in the neighbourhood on a private matter.'

His host made no response, but sipped his drink. Hardy was aware of an almost overwhelming rage building inside him. He put it down to fatigue following the journey. He looked around the room as he fought to get a grip on his temper. At last he said, 'I'm not quite sure how I can be of service to you. I'm certain you're aware that the Metropolitan police have no powers on this side of the border. If you need help with a criminal matter, may I recommend you get in touch with the local procurator fiscal.'

With a loud sound that didn't bode well for the crystal, his host set down his glass on a side-table. He took several steps forward until he was a bare foot from Hardy. And drew himself up straight as if attempting to match Hardy's height but failing by a matter of three inches. He stared right into Hardy's face in a manner designed to intimidate, then said softly between his teeth, 'Now look here, laddie. Don't give me any of your insubordination. I am perfectly aware of the legal situation vis á vis English police and Scottish law. I do not need you to acquaint me with the procedures for criminal investigation. I am perfectly capable of contacting the local procurator fiscal as and when I see fit, since that gentleman is my closest friend. In future I would suggest you remember your place before treating your superiors to a lecture. For your further information, I am also perfectly able to contact your senior officer and have you dismissed. Is that clear?'

Before Hardy could comment, not that he had anything to say that wouldn't result in the immediate cessation of his career with the Metropolitan police, the man continued with, 'I am Howard Denholme, laird of this estate, and I don't mind telling you, Hardy, that your conduct this evening is not calculated to impress. I shall be having a word with my good friend, the assistant commander of the Metropolitan police. I may say, thus far, you are a disgrace to the service. An utter disgrace. Therefore, do me the favour of speaking with my butler concerning the 'criminal matter', as you put it, before I kick your contemptible backside from here to kingdom come.'

Blushing with embarrassment and unabated rage, Hardy uttered a stiff and largely inadequate apology, but before he could withdraw, someone tapped on the study door, and slowly opened it. An elegant lady, very slender and small, came into the room. She stayed by the door, her hands clasped in front of her.

'Pardon me,' she said to Hardy, who offered her a smile and a slight bow.

'Not at all. I was just leaving.' He went out, shutting the door behind him very slowly. As he did so, he heard her say,

'You wished to see me?'

Mr Denholme, still in a temper, began to shout very loudly about something that had got broken.

Hardy turned to the butler who was hovering nearby. 'The governess? Or the housekeeper?'

The butler gave a derisive snort. 'Believe it or not, that was the lady of the house, Mrs Denholme.'

Hardy was astonished. Yet he had seen those signs before: the large overbearing husband, the tiny, frightened, birdlike wife. It was an arrangement that never ended well. He shook his head to rid it of the image of her soft anxious eyes, the clasping hands.

The butler was leading him to the back of the house. At the bottom of a flight of dimly-lit, uncarpeted stairs, he stepped aside to wave Hardy into a room.

'Come into my parlour, said the spider to the fly.'

Hardy smiled at the cliché. 'Thank you. Tell me, is this an inherited lairdship?'

The butler waved him into a seat, and responded with another snort. 'Nah, he bought it, didn't he. When he made his first million from his boot polish empire.'

'Interesting.'

'You and me are in the wrong job, mate,' the butler added. Hardy couldn't disagree with that.

Upstairs, Louisa Denholme came out of the study trembling but resolute. She went to the telephone in the hall. She had to be quick. Her fingers trembled as she held the receiver and asked the operator for a number. At the other end of the line, the bell rang and eventually, as she was on the verge of giving up for fear of being caught, someone answered. 'Ah, Mr Nelson...' she began.

'Milk and sugar, Inspector?'

Hardy roused himself from his inner thoughts, going over and over the scene that had just taken place in the study. 'Er, yes please, one sugar. Thank you.'

Mr Roberts was a Londoner through and through. He added the merest splash of milk and a generous teaspoon of sugar then passed the cup to Hardy. Taking his own cup, the butler came to sit opposite Hardy in a worn but comfortable armchair.

'Do you miss London?' Hardy asked. Roberts laughed.

'What, miss all that noise? Not to mention the dirt, smog and traffic? Of course I do! Stuck up here with the heather and the trees and the hills. It's like being in the bleedin' jungle, if you ask me. Eagles the size of a small pony buzzing past every five minutes. I miss the sparrers. You can't put out breadcrumbs for a bleedin' eagle, let me tell you! Take your bleedin' arm off, I don't doubt.' He stirred his cup noisily, allowing the teaspoon to clatter into the saucer. Then he took a loud slurp of his tea and sat back with an appreciative sigh. 'It's just one of many reasons why the locals hate Mr Denholme. I've got to admit, I can see their point. He ought to have given employment to the local people first, then to outsiders. But he never. He's got some funny ideas. He sees this place as a little slice of English heaven, nestled right in under their Jacobite noses. His words, not mine. My missus is a Scot and I wouldn't say a word against 'em.'

Hardy drank his tea, burning his mouth in doing so. He set the cup aside. 'In what way are his ideas 'funny'?'

'Well, he sees it as his duty to be a proud Englishman wherever he goes. He gets peoples' backs up more than just a bit. He even gets provisions sent up from London by train then horse and cart from the station, and yours truly isn't the only one here what's an outsider. I mean, I hope I'm as patriotic as the next man. I done my bit during the Great War, fought for King and country, with my fellow soldiers—many of them Scots, and Irish, or the Taffies from the Welsh valleys, even them black fellows what come over from Jamaica and out that way, lots of Caribbean chappies, freezing their socks off in Belgium along with the rest of us. Then there was Aussies, Kiwis. Like brothers, we all was. Good men all of them, never let me down, knew I could trust them with my life. In fact, I did trust them with me life, and proud to do it. Er—what was I saying?'

'You did your bit for your country,' Hardy said.

'Ah, yes. Proud to do it, proud. But well, it's just my opinion but what His Nibs takes it a bit too far. Not that I'd be mug enough to say it to his face. He don't like to be disagreed with, our Mr D. Out like a shot I'd be, if he knew. Plus he's a bit chippy, if you know what I mean. Because he bought his way in, and he don't really fit. Likes to wield his power.'

'Hmm.' Hardy looked around him. The room was cosy and well-lit, though the wallpaper was somewhat faded, and here and there a corner of the paper curled back a little from the wall. A crack ran up the wall around the doorframe. An attempt had been made to fill it with crushed paper and a touch of paint, but the crack had widened. Beyond the butler's sitting room, there was the kitchen, not that you'd know it was there if you didn't see it, there was almost no noise coming from that direction, though now and again he saw a woman in an apron go along the dark hallway. On his left, he could see out into the garden through a large picture window, the light from the house illuminating a patch of grass that he took to be the beginning of a lawn.

There was a lull. Pleasant though it was to be sitting there, especially now his foul mood was starting to evaporate, he felt he'd better get down to business. At some point he'd love to get to his bed.

'So what is the problem at the moment here? Why was I needed? I was told you could—er—put me in the picture.'

'Well, there's been two break-ins, and there's been threats. There was nearly a fire though Mr Denholme caught it just in time and managed to put it out. There's been trouble with vandals, poachers, you name it, it's been going on for the last month or so. It's like some kind of vendetta against the family.'

'Tell me about the fire.'

'There's not much to tell. One morning a fire started in the little sitting room. We took it that a piece of wood fell out of the fire onto the hearth rug. Mrs Denholme discovered it, and raised the alarm. Mr Denholme, he just marched in there and stamped it out. A bit risky, that, though I suppose I'd have done more damage with me bucket o' water.'

'Hmm,' said Hardy, 'Much damage?'

'Needed a new hearth rug. A lick of paint on the wall one side of the fireplace. Nothing too serious. Could have been far worse if it had gone unnoticed.'

'What about the other matters? Anything taken during these break-ins?'

'Spare cash from Mr Denholme's desk drawer. Only about forty quid, a decent amount, but not worth hanging for.'

'Very true.'

'A few bits of jewellery. A few knick-knacks, small but pricey stuff. I believe there was a silver cup, one that was awarded to Mr Denholme for some golfing tournament a year or two back. Mrs Denholme's pearls. The usual stuff.'

Hardy nodded, looking about him again. The theft had hardly yielded a large haul. The large house was somewhat shabby in appearance. These things together made him suspicious.

'I see. Did you see or hear any of these threats? What were they, letters?'

'No, I didn't see them. I was just told about them.

They was pushed under the French doors in the study; the doors don't fit too well. One note came last week, one the week before, and one before that. Mr Denholme did say he burned them to avoid her ladyship or the children seeing them. 'Vile language' was what he told me. What was going to be done to him and his lady if they didn't get out, that kind of thing. 'Course he got rid of the first one, so as not to upset Mrs Denholme, but not thinking there might be more. But then two more came and he had to get rid of them as well. Said they contained the same kind of threat, 'You're for it. Get out or else', same as before.'

'Do you know of anyone in particular who has a grudge against Mr Denholme?'

'Got a queue about a mile long, if you ask me. Anyone hereabouts who's out of work, or one of the masses that's been sacked or fined or evicted or sent to prison. Oh, he's been busy locally, has Mr Denholme, and he's bosom pals with the procurator fiscal. If you ask the constable in the next village, he can probably give you the names of a few local villains. Just stand well back when you tell anyone yours, is my advice.' He chuckled at that but declined to be drawn into an explanation.

Hardy thanked him for the tea and left, deep in thought. He went through to the kitchen and spent ten minutes talking to the rest of the staff—the butler's wife who was the cook, and a young girl who assisted her and did some cleaning, under the title of maid-of-all-work. They were still trying to get all the dinner things washed, dried and put away. A stray cloth, dropped on the back of a chair, showed that Mr Roberts had been helping when Hardy had arrived.

'Is this the whole staff?' Hardy queried. 'It's not many for a house this size.'

'Aye weel, he let two go last week, said their work wasnae up to scratch. And one last month for the same reason. Then there were three more lost over the previous few months, not that we are privy to the reasons why. So now it's just us, expected to run ourselves ragged keeping this place together,' Mrs Roberts told him.

He thought that was curious. But it added weight to his initial idea.

Just at that moment, Mrs Denholme came into the kitchen. He introduced himself now, having not done so on their first meeting. She seemed flustered, which he put down to her surprise at meeting a London policeman in her own kitchen. However, she was friendly and personable, unlike her husband, and so small in stature he felt an instinctive urge to protect her. He explained why he was there, and she thanked him for his help, adding that she realised it wasn't his province, but that she knew her husband was worried about the general spite against him, and would be glad of Hardy's assistance. Hardy himself had his doubts, but he simply smiled and promised to do all he could.

He asked her if she had seen anyone hanging about the place at any time, or had any idea who might be behind the incidents. She turned pale at the mention of them, and he wasn't surprised. She seemed a timid little thing and no doubt she found it all very alarming. But she said she couldn't help him.

'I'm sorry, Inspector, but I try to keep out of my husband's business affairs. My sphere is very much the traditional one of home and children. And now, please, do excuse me, Inspector,' Mrs Denholme said. 'I'm afraid I only came down to collect a hot water bottle for my youngest son, it's a little chilly in the nursery. So I must bid you good evening.'

The maid passed over a filled rubber bottle and Mrs Denholme, clasping the bottle to her front, as if it were she and not the child who was cold, turned away and went back upstairs.

'A very pleasant lady,' he commented to the cook.

She nodded and smiled, 'Aye, she's sweetness herself, that one. How she puts up with that man, I don't know, but still...'

'Indeed.' Hardy made a mental note. He asked the maid and the cook if they had noticed anything out of the ordinary, seen or heard anything at all to give any clue to the identity of the burglar or writer of the threatening notes. But they told him they hadn't noticed anyone hanging about, hadn't seen the notes, hadn't heard any gossip in the village. Unable to think of anything else worth asking just then, Hardy said goodbye and left.

Gregg appeared from nowhere to accompany him back to the village. At first Hardy had been going to tell him there was no need, but then he remembered the horse and cart.

He would have to contact the constable in the morning, as the butler had suggested. Then he would need to try to arrange a meeting with the procurator fiscal as a matter of courtesy to explain his presence, as well as to discuss the concerns of his best friend, the laird. That would be a meeting he needed to handle with the utmost tact and discretion, two resources he always felt he distinctly lacked.

It was just after half past ten when he finally reached his room. He had a bath in lukewarm water and got changed, thinking to go downstairs to find the landlord and see whether he had heard any gossip about Mr Denholme's problems. But suddenly weary, he lay down on his bed, fully clothed, and at once fell asleep.

He was not allowed to sleep for long, however. Almost immediately, or so it seemed to him, someone began to pound on his door, calling out in a thunderous voice fit to wake the dead, 'Hardy? Are you there? William Hardy!'

From across the corridor came an answering yap from the Pekinese in one another of the guest rooms.

Drunk with weariness, Hardy stumbled to the door, only managing to call out a quick, 'Yes, yes, I'm coming, I'm coming,' as he fumbled with the lock and the handle.

The door opened almost of its own volition, and as Hardy looked up, bewildered, he had only time to note a large man filling the doorway before the man's fist connected with Hardy's cheek and everything went black.

*

Day Three: Thursday

After the events of the previous evening, Hardy was convinced he'd struggle to get up in the morning. But he had reckoned without the assistance of a nearby cockerel that woke him every two minutes from half past three. By six o'clock that morning, Hardy was ready to kill the bird and eat it for breakfast. At the very least, he hoped it would be on the evening's menu. Clearly, he had become a city boy. No doubt the locals could happily sleep through the sounds of the country, but he found them intrusive and surprisingly loud. So much for the 'peace and quiet' of rural life.

His head pounded. His right eye was partially closed and surrounded by a halo of purple following the visit from the unknown assailant the previous night. He remembered nothing after going to the door. He could picture his hand on the doorknob, but after that, he had no memory of what had happened. But he was going to do his damnedest to find out.

He felt weary to the core, but with so much to do, and that blasted bird squawking, lying in bed was not an option. There was no hot water, so he washed and shaved in cold, and swallowed a couple of aspirin. By the time he reached the small room where the inn's guests ate their meals, he was not in the best of moods.

The unmistakable smell of kippers met his nostrils as he pushed open the door. One glance inside showed him the same elderly woman from the night before, passing bits of kipper to the fat Pekinese standing on a chair beside her. The smell intensified, and the sight of the dog slurping chunks of kipper off the table turned Hardy's stomach. He left the room without so much as a greeting, and went into the bar to see if the landlord was about.

'Ah, Inspector. And how are you this morning?' Nelson was already polishing glasses. Did he ever do anything else, Hardy wondered.

'Good morning,' Hardy said. 'If it is a good morning. I'm not feeling at my best, I think it's fair to say. I'm sure you know by now that I was attacked in my room last night. Is this a common occurrence, would you say? I'm not quite sure why you didn't call the police.'

At the mention of police, Nelson looked alarmed. He set down his cloth and glass, and with an understanding smile and calming-down gestures with his hands, said, 'Aye, aye, I know sir, and I'm very, very sorry. Unfortunately, no one noticed who went up to your room, but it wasnae very late, and the bar here was open; it's open to the public, as I'm sure you realise. I will of course, knock a night's accommodation off your bill.'

'Very generous of you, I'm sure,' Hardy's tone was sarcastic but Nelson took it as genuine thanks.

The landlord said with misplaced attempt at humour, 'Everyone'll think your wife did that to ye.'

'It's not good enough,' Hardy pointed out. 'I was in bed asleep, someone pounded on my door, I got up and opened it, and then...'

'Aye, and I'm truly sorry, as I said. The noise woke our lady novelist, which is how I got involved. And a good thing I did. The doctor was drinking in the bar, so I brought him straight up to have a wee look at you. See, I made sure you had medical attention as soon as could be,' Nelson emphasised, as if he'd done all that could be reasonably expected. He went on to tell Hardy that the elderly woman had puffed downstairs in the largest nightdress he had ever seen, her revolting dog yapping continually at her heels. The woman had reported hearing 'a brawl', then proceeded to demand a discount on her bill because of the disturbance. The landlord and doctor had hurried upstairs, but they hadn't seen the assailant, and Nelson was unable to shed any further light on the identity of Hardy's visitor.

'Obviously someone knew I was here,' Hardy said sourly.

'Aye. No doubt it's all over the village that a William Hardy is staying at The Thistle.'

Clearly the whole thing was a waste of time, but Hardy couldn't help adding, 'And that bloody chicken next door didn't help matters any. I hope it will be on the menu for dinner tonight.'

Peter Nelson chuckled. Hardy had not been joking, but there was no point in pursuing the matter. No doubt tonight he'd be too deeply asleep to notice. At least, he hoped so.

Nelson said, 'My wife's got a nice casserole planned for this evening, but it won't be chicken. Although...' He leaned closer, and dropping his voice, even though no one else was in the vicinity, he said, 'Look, if anyone asks, perhaps you wouldn't mind saying it was a chicken casserole, sir. Ye ken? Chicken, don't ye forget now. Never say what it really was.'

Hardy stared at him. Was Nelson seriously saying that to a policeman? He stared at the landlord for a full minute, before giving up and nodding his understanding. There was no point in getting involved in that little problem too.

He went outside, got in his car and drove along the coast road until he found somewhere to get something to eat. By nine o'clock he was knocking on the front door of the police house in the next village.

'Did your wife do that to you, laddie?' Constable Forbes asked as Hardy came in. Howard Denholme had also called Hardy 'laddie', but coming from the plump constable with the genial smile, this time it didn't feel like a deliberate insult. Hardy guessed Forbes was approaching retirement age, although his round face was as smooth and unlined as it had no doubt been forty years earlier.

They'd come into what was essentially the front parlour of a home, though with a desk and a few chairs and a filing cabinet. An array of wet-weather gear and ropes was bundled on a tired-looking coat stand in the corner.

In the glass of the window, darkened by a large rambling plant outside, Hardy caught sight of his face with the huge purple bruise that spread across the upper part of his cheek and surrounded his right, partially-closed eye. He thought ruefully that he certainly didn't look like a police officer.

'Er, no.' He refused to be drawn into an explanation, as he still had no real idea who had attacked him, or why. That was yet another thing he'd have to deal with later. Instead he pulled out his warrant card to identify himself, and said, 'I'm Inspector William Hardy of the Metropolitan police. I'm in the area on private business, but last night I was called to Mr Howard Denholme's residence—er—Barr Hall. I expect you know the place, and the family. I understand they have been having a few problems lately. Do you know anything about that at all?'

This was all ignored except the first part of his speech. The police constable stared at him in astonishment.

'I'm sorry, sir, what did you say your name was?'

Impatiently Hardy held the warrant card out so the constable could see for himself. The constable took it, held it to the light of the barred, shadowed window, and examined it for a full two minutes. Hardy, exhausted physically and mentally, was on the point of losing his temper. He made a strong effort to rein himself in. He wouldn't get anywhere if he lost his temper. He said, as politely as he could, 'Is there some kind of problem, Constable?'

The constable immediately returned the warrant card, and in a belated attempt to show due respect, practically snapped to attention. 'Not at all, sir. There you are, sir. Sorry, sir, I didn't quite catch...'

With a sigh, Hardy repeated his query regarding Howard Denholme. The constable still didn't look as if he was listening. Instinctively, Hardy knew the man was still pondering the warrant card. Clearly they wouldn't get anywhere until he dealt with whatever issue that had created.

'What is it?' he asked, trying to sound patient, and failing miserably.

'Och, no sir, it's nothing, nothing at all. What can I do for you?'

'Well, I've already told you twice, that I'm...'

'It's just that you've the very same name and the very same face as one of our most notorious local petty criminals.'

'...here about Mr Denholme's... I'm sorry, what did you say?' Hardy stared at the constable.

Constable Forbes shifted his feet and looked as though he wished for the ground to open up and swallow him. 'Well sir, not meaning any disrespect, but we've got a young fellow in the neighbourhood, and he's also called William Hardy. He's recently been released from a year in prison for theft, and he's already up to his old tricks: poaching, petty theft, receiving stolen goods, drunken brawling, and of course, his own personal favourite, seducing other men's wives. And he could be your twin brother if it wasn't for your nice suit.'

Hardy, tempted to ask the constable to repeat himself, simply paused for a moment to mull this information over. Could this possibly be the reason he had been attacked? A simple case of mistaken identity? Not that this made it excusable.

'Here? Or in Lower Bar?'

'Well, he gets about a bit. I'm not quite sure exactly where he's staying, but mostly he's active in Lower Bar. Like as not he's sleeping rough somewhere.'

Common sense reasserted itself. Hardy shrugged. 'I suppose it's scarcely the most unusual name, is it? My first name is probably one of the commonest in Britain, and the surname is hardly rare. Now, if we could just get back to my request?'

'Yes sir, of course. Er, what was that again?'

Hardy drove into Edinburgh to see the procurator fiscal, only to find the great man was not available.

He was informed by the gentleman's secretary that he needed to make an appointment. An appointment not being available until the following week, eventually the secretary agreed to arrange a telephone call to Hardy later at the inn. It seemed that the eminent gentleman might be able to spare three minutes to speak with Hardy.

He returned to Lower Bar, irritable and frustrated at the delay. He had a lukewarm, gritty coffee at The Thistle whilst he awaited the call from the procurator fiscal's office. When it finally came through, an hour later than the time agreed, the essence of the call was that the procurator had a vague idea that Mr Denholme had mentioned his troubles, but it had been during a golf match with a number of others, and they hadn't the leisure to discuss anything in detail. He added that he was ignorant of whether or not Mr Denholme had elected to speak to the police in Edinburgh about the issue.

That appeared to be the end of the case, as far as the procurator was concerned. Some friend, Hardy thought. The procurator was really not at all interested in Mr Denholme's affairs. Perhaps Mr Denholme was simply claiming a friendship that in truth did not extend beyond mere acquaintance?

Hardy came out of the inn's little back office feeling unenlightened. How had he come to be mixed up in all this mess? At the back of his mind, a little voice said, 'For £500 and the chance of asking Dottie Manderson to be your wife.' With his lack of progress in all areas, he felt as though a cloud of gloom had settled over him. His mood did not improve when he saw the smiling eager face of Mr Gregg from the Hall, ready for his first driving lesson in the motor car.

Gregg's benign gaze took in the damage sustained by Hardy's face, and looking him straight in the eye, he asked, 'Did your wife do that to you, laddie?'

After the driving lesson, his nerves frayed, his stomach unsettled, and in desperate need of fresh air, Hardy decided to have a walk around the village. This took him ten minutes. A second walk made it twenty. He was still mulling over the problems Howard Denholme was experiencing. Should he, in fact, go to the police in Edinburgh, and see if they were investigating on Denholme's behalf, or should he simply give the whole thing up as a mare's nest? After all, he was on annual leave, and had no jurisdiction here. Undecided, he walked around the village again, then spent a further twenty minutes looking around the church and its graveyard, which only succeeded in making him depressed as he thought of his mother and her recent passing. He went down the street to look at the sea, but the beach was rocky and perilous, and he couldn't actually reach the water's edge.

He returned to The Thistle and put through a phone call to his own office in London. He was greatly comforted to hear the familiar robust tones of Sergeant Maple, his assistant and close friend. After exchanging news for the first two minutes, Hardy had then to squeeze a lot into the final minute, asking Maple to find out if anyone had been sent to Lower Bar from the Met, as it seemed he—or someone from the Met—had been expected. Then he asked Maple to find out anything he could about Howard Denholme.

By twelve o'clock Hardy had run out of things to do. He decided that a change was as good as a rest, and crossing the road, he walked along to the other pub, which bore the name The Dirk. He wondered if they offered lunches.

The door opened directly into a dim bar. Coming in out of the bright sunshine, he could see little in the gloom and collided with a large body.

'Who are you?' a voice demanded before he could apologise.

With no thought for his personal safety, for the second time he gave a stranger his name. He said, 'William Hardy.' He had just enough time to see a large fist coming at him out of the shadows, then stars spun before his eyes and he knew no more.

He awoke a little while later. The first thing he was aware of was the pounding in his head. Then he realised he was lying down in a dark room. Opening his left eye with extreme caution, he recognised his suitcase lying on the dresser beside the bed. He was back in his room at the inn, then. There was a cold damp cloth over his forehead, and someone had pulled off his shoes and set them neatly beside the bed. His shirt collar had been loosened, his tie was draped over the bed rail. Moving his head to get a better look proved to be a mistake. Pain drove him back against the cool linen cover of the pillow, his hands going up to protect his face and explore the damage he had sustained.

His nose felt twice its usual size, and was crusted with dried blood. It was tender, and even the gentlest touch sent agony flaring through him.

Dottie had chosen to travel up to Scotland on the Flying Scotsman from Kings Cross at ten o'clock in the morning, just twenty-four hours after William Hardy. Not that she knew that, of course.

Dottie got out her knitting. She was still making little garments for Flora's baby. So far she had made four matinee jackets, four pairs of leggings, six pairs of mittens and bootees, one shawl and was now making a set of little vests in the second size. It was rather difficult to believe that an actual person would very soon wear the garments she had been making. It just didn't seem possible. From what Flora had said, Dottie knew her sister felt equally surprised by the idea.

Dottie herself hoped to have children some day—in spite of the little she knew about the actual process of giving birth—and she had found it illuminating to watch her sister's pregnancy progressing, seeing how her sister coped, and how her brother-in-law reacted, so protective and loving towards his wife. She was surprised at how interested George was in the mundane details of the pregnancy. Dottie had assumed that no man would get involved until the child was old enough to play trains with or to take fishing. And, due to her fairly new attachment to William Hardy, she had been thinking a good deal about marriage and babies of late.

At the New Year ball at George's parents house, she had chatted with George's sister Diana, who had expressed some fairly elevated views about husbands and children, and the duties of being a wife. Dottie hadn't exactly agreed with everything that Diana said, but she understood and even sympathised with the emotions behind the words. But Diana had been having an illicit affair with a man who was murdered. So how would Diana be feeling now about her dreams of being a dutiful and loving wife and mother?

How odd life was, Dottie thought. One minute you were an adolescent who giggled and blushed at the slightest suggestion of romance, the next you were a woman approaching the birth of your first child, and it was all about practical details of preparing the nursery.

She thought about her errand. She'd thought of little else since Mr Bray had explained it to her. She wondered what kind of reception she would get from the man she'd come here to find. Once she had found him, of course. She had been told to expect a message the following afternoon to tell her where and when to meet her contact, who would in turn lead her to Mrs Carmichael's long-lost son. It was all a bit cloak and dagger, and not for the first time, she thought it seemed oddly out of character for the always very forthright Mrs Carmichael.

What did you say to someone who had never known their mother? What good would it do, if all you could tell them was that the mother they'd never known was now dead? It was too late for him to know her. Too late to have a relationship with her. There would be no memories to share. No searching her face to see if you had her nose, her eyes. What was the point now of this? And yet, it was what Mrs Carmichael had wanted. Mr Bray had told Dottie only a little about the various other legacies. Perhaps some part of the woman's estate had been bequeathed to her son? Would that comfort him, to know his mother had wanted to help him with her wealth? Or would he be angry or jealous that Dottie had inherited the warehouse and so much more?

Mrs Carmichael had suffered from not knowing her child. Had it been a consolation to know he was out there, somewhere, living his life, learning to walk and talk, going to school, growing up? He'd probably be married by now, perhaps with children: grandchildren Mrs Carmichael would never see. It broke Dottie's heart to think of it. Mrs Carmichael had always been so interested in other people's children and romances. Surely that showed how much she missed her only child?

By the time Dottie reached Edinburgh that evening, she was exhausted by her emotions. Her head was swimming with the continual passing of scenery, which by the end of the journey, she could see even when she closed her eyes.

Following dinner in a rather grand hotel in Edinburgh, she found Mr Bray had kindly reserved a taxi to drive her to the village of Lower Bar. She was grateful for the convenience though felt frustrated by yet another journey where she had to remain seated. At least it was dark outside, and she did not have to attend to yet more lovely countryside. The taxi driver chatted to her amiably though she only caught one word in ten, his rich accent drowned by the noisy engine of his motor car. Her replies were mainly in the form of nods and smiles. The journey consisted almost entirely of sharp upward or horizontal bends and quite a lot of getting out to open or close gates. She began to wonder if the cabbie had taken a short cut across some private estate; that seemed only too possible from the twisting route they were taking to the village.

But at last she arrived. The first thing she noted was the fresh salty air and the sound of the sea softly moving beyond the high dunes at the end of the street. As she got out and paid the driver, she looked about her. She was not able to make out very much. There seemed to be no streetlamps in Lower Bar, and most of the homes had no light on, or showed only the gleam of a lamp through thick curtains. The hotel, which was not in her opinion a true hotel— quite clearly it was just a pub—only had one small light by its front door, illuminating a tattered sign declaring that this was, 'The Thistle'.

The taxi driver lifted out Dottie's luggage and prepared to carry it into the hotel for her. She touched his arm, and he turned and looked back at her.

'Is there anywhere else?' she asked, trying to keep her voice down. Her scalp prickled. She felt as though she were being watched. 'I don't mind paying for you to take me somewhere else. I'm just not sure...'

'There's no another hotel for a couple of miles, Missie, but I can run you back into Edinburgh if you'd like.' He watched her closely, waiting whilst she made her decision. She bit her lip, and looked about her. She felt stuck, unable to make up her mind. The horrid sense of being watched persisted. She began to feel that even in daylight, she wouldn't like Lower Bar very much. Yet she had given Mr Bray her word.

Tiredness washed over her. All at once she decided that she couldn't be bothered. All she wanted was a cup of hot tea and to get to bed.

'I'm sorry,' she said. 'That would be silly, wouldn't it? I'll stay here as planned. I'm sure it's perfectly pleasant.'

The cabbie looked about him with an air of astonishment. 'I wouldnae be too sure.' But he gave her a reassuring smile, and told her how to reach him if she changed her mind.

Oddly, being armed with this information fortified her spirits, and she nodded, confident that she'd made the right choice. 'I'll stay. It'll be perfectly all right. Thank you!' she added. She did just glance back over her shoulder. In the shadows of a large spreading tree along the street, she could make out the jut of a shoulder and the tall outline of a man. An intermittent soft red glow told her he was smoking a cigarette. He was watching her. With a light laugh that didn't quite work, she said to the cabbie, 'I see the local spy has already spotted me.'

The cabbie carried her suitcase into the hotel, she said goodbye to him and went inside.

Inside it was at least warm, if not quite of the standard she'd been hoping. Heavy dark brown panelling, deer heads and antlers adorned every wall. Dusty glass cases of stuffed fish, birds and pine martens cluttered every shelf and tabletop. The whole effect was one of deep Victorian gloom.

Dottie quickly discovered there was no reception area as such, she had to go into the bar to sign in the book and collect her room key. Just five rooms in all, she noted, and two already taken. The innkeeper introduced himself as Peter Nelson, and seemed friendly enough. Better still, he was expecting her. By now it was almost ten o'clock, and she was weary to the bone.

'My wife'll bring you hot soup to your room in ten minutes, ma'am. Is there anything else you'll be wanting? Perhaps a wee dram to get you off to sleep?'

Dottie smothered a laugh. What would her mother say if she knew that Dottie had been putting away whisky? She thanked the man and told him the soup would be very welcome, and asked for a pot of tea. 'If it's not too much trouble,' she added.

'No trouble at all,' he told her. 'And if I could just find ma son, we'll get your suitcase taken up to your room. That boy is never here when I need him. Off out at all hours of the night, too, getting himself into trouble.'

'Oh dear,' Dottie said, with a polite smile. 'That sounds just like all the young chaps today.' Then, whilst they waited, she said, 'You have other guests staying in the hotel, I imagine?'

'Aye that we do. We only have a few rooms, but they are often full.'

He didn't seem inclined to say any more about his guests. Just then a tall gangly lad appeared, casting a glower at his father.

'Well, laddie, take the lady's suitcase up to room three. And no more of your disappearing tricks, I need your help this evening.'

The boy grabbed her suitcase as if it weighed nothing, and ran up the stairs with it two at a time. Dottie took her key and thanking Mr Nelson, she went upstairs. By the time she reached room three, the door was standing open and her suitcase had been placed at the foot of her bed. The young man was on his way back out. She thanked him, and he bobbed his head at her in a kind of partial bow.

'I'm Alex Nelson. That's my dad you spoke to downstairs,' he said. And blushing slightly as she smiled at him, he added, 'If you need anything more, Miss, just you call me.'

She thanked him again, though not quite sure how he would hear her if she called out for him from her room. But it was the thought that counted. So far, all her doubts about the place had been allayed. Though as she unpacked her belongings and waited for the soup, she couldn't help thinking about the smoking man lurking outside.

She found it hard to sleep in a strange new place. She'd had her soup, watery and almost cold, accompanied by heavy, dry bread, and was beginning to think her initial thoughts of finding somewhere else to stay had been correct after all. This place was going to be awful. She sat by the window looking out into the quiet village street. At least it seemed that the smoking man had gone. The noise from the bar across the road had died down. She'd seen several men leave, totteringly helping one another along the road to their homes. The only other person she saw was a stout elderly dog-walker, wearing a raincoat over her nightgown, impatiently pulling a reluctant fat little dog along. Dottie carefully unpacked all her belongings. Then she found the book she had brought with her and settled down to read it.

About an hour later, Howard Denholme was in his study. He looked up on hearing a tap at the door, and called out his characteristically imperious, 'Come.'

The door opened, someone came into the room, approaching the desk with caution. A light breeze blew in at the open door to the garden, causing the curtains to flutter and flare out a little, dancing on the air. From beyond the door, the sound of squabbling rooks, raucous and unmelodic, broke upon the silence.

The person halted just short of the bearskin. 'You sent for me?'

Mr Denholme came round the desk, his cold rage well in hand. Only his pale countenance revealed his true feelings. 'Did you honestly think I wouldn't demand an explanation? Did you honestly think I wouldn't hear about what was going on? Did you...'

He managed no more. There was no time for him to think or to act. A slight sound, followed by a very loud one, and he fell like a stone, that habitual expression of disgust etched permanently on his features.

*

Day Four: Friday

Another day and another early start, thanks to the pain of his injuries, and once again, the racket from the cockerel next door. Hardy could hardly bear to dab a washcloth on his face due to the extreme tenderness of his nose, cheekbone and eye. He managed to shave, dismissing the notion of growing a beard just to save effort. Hopefully a smooth chin would offset the other less attractive aspects of his face. He had no desire to look more like a drunken thug than he could help.

He couldn't remember when he had last eaten, but there was no way on earth he could face kippers or porridge. A short drive into the nearest town, and he had provided himself with some cold meat and fruit for his breakfast from a market stall just setting up. Next he drove to Constable Forbes's police house to scrounge some coffee, or if absolutely necessary, tea. And he was very glad he did so, because he was right there sitting at the table when the telephone call came through at a few minutes to seven.

Twenty minutes later, he approached the body that lay half on the polished wooden boards of the floor, and half on the bearskin rug. The man lay stretched out on his back, his arms by his sides, his legs crossed at the ankles. It was immediately clear he had been blasted at close range in the abdomen with some kind of firearm, almost certainly a shotgun, to judge by the mess, Hardy thought. The man's eyes were open but dull, his face clean and undamaged. His frozen expression was not unlike the look of disgusted scorn he had directed at Hardy the evening before last. Blood soaked the tatters of the man's shirt and waistcoat, plastering the cloth to the body, a very inadequate dressing on the massive wound. Here and there the blood was still red and liquid, but for the most part it was now brown and almost dry.

Blood had spilt onto the floor, running down the minute cracks between the boards. It had seeped and splashed across the bearskin, leaving the extinct beast's fur mottled with dark, damp patches. There were splashes of blood and fragments of human tissue on the wall immediately behind the desk, a thick trail of blood had run down to the floor. Fine particles frosted the surfaces of a large area of the wall and the glass of two pictures as if sprayed there with a tube and misting-bulb, such as one found on a perfume bottle. But rather than fragrant, the air in the room was foul with the stench of blood and death.

'Has anyone touched him?' he asked Mr Roberts. The butler, pale but composed, shook his head.

'No sir, we didn't let Mrs Denholme enter the room, or either of the children of course. The only ones what's been in here is myself and the maid. You met her yesterday. It was her as found Mr Denholme when she came in to do the fire at half past six this morning. She fetched me and I came in to see for myself. Not that I didn't believe her, it just seemed impossible that such a thing... But there. As soon as I saw him, I knew there couldn't be no doubt that he was dead.'

'Hmm.' Hardy began to look about the room. There was every appearance of a disturbance. A door to a small cupboard in the corner was standing open, as was the door of the empty safe inside. The drawers of the desk had been ripped out—one was even lying broken and upside down on the floor beside the desk—the papers in disarray all over the rug behind the desk. The desk-lamp had been knocked over and the green glass shade smashed. Miniscule green shards confettied the floor.

'Did Mr Denholme have any visitors last night?'

'No one came to the front door, sir. As far as I'm aware no one came near the house all night.'

'I imagine you would have come into the study in the latter part of the evening?'

'Yes sir, I came in to make up the fire at about ten o'clock, and to ask if there was anything else I could do. Mr Denholme was alone, sir, and sat at his desk reading a letter.'

The grate was cold now, and still waiting to be cleared out and made up. Ash had spilled all over the hearth and even onto the rug, Hardy noticed. He said:

'A letter that he had written, or that he had received?'

'Received, sir. The envelope, a big brown one it was, was lying beside his elbow, and I recognised the stamps and the handwriting from an item of post that arrived yesterday morning.'

'Did you recognise the writing?'

'No sir. All I remember is that it was very neat and loopy.' He described a few curving letters in the air. 'The postmark was London. But I don't remember anything else.'

There was no large brown envelope there now. Hardy had a quick look through the papers on the floor, and on the desk. He made a mental note to check in the other rooms, as soon as he was able to procure a warrant, although glancing back at the fireplace, he thought it was pretty clear where the envelope had gone.

'I see. Thank you, Mr Roberts. Did you hear anything at all? Any disturbance, shouting, hear anyone running from the house?'

'No sir, nothing.'

Hardy watched him closely. 'Really? Nothing at all? You didn't hear someone discharging a firearm, presumably a shotgun, inside the house late last night?'

Albert Roberts fidgeted and looked at his feet briefly before meeting Hardy's stare with one of defiance. 'No sir, nothing. We was all in bed. It's a big house, and the staff bedrooms are three floors up in the attic, and at the front of the house, whereas this room faces out to the back. We knew nothing about it until this morning, and I called the constable immediately I saw Mr Denholme was dead.'

Hardy nodded. 'Very well, thank you, Mr Roberts, you've been very helpful. I was there when the call came through, so I can confirm the time the crime was reported. Constable Forbes will contact everyone we'll need. I'm afraid there will be a number of people arriving at the house shortly. No doubt the constable himself will be along too.'

'Yes sir. When I rang earlier, he said he would

notify the Edinburgh police. And I expect the ambulance will be along very soon.'

'Indeed. But Mr Denholme's body can't be moved,' Hardy reminded him, just in case it wasn't perfectly clear. 'No one can touch the body or move it. Not until photographs have been taken, and the rest of the necessary evidence collected. Also, a police doctor will need to examine the body.'

If anything, Mr Roberts went even paler, but he simply nodded, saying nothing.

There were footprints on the floor. They came across the corner of the terrace outside from the cover of a shrubbery that screened the back of the house from the road to the garages. The footprints—still slightly muddy—tracked up the step, in at the open garden door, across the small patch of flooring then appeared briefly on the edge of the rug by the desk. Another pair of prints showed very neatly on the floor not three feet from the head of the deceased.

'I will be asking the procurator for a search warrant. I want to try to find that letter you told me about. It may be that our intruder came here just for that. Though it's possible Mr Denholme had burned it. However, the procurator fiscal will probably have to call in a proxy or a fiscal from another area, seeing that he and the deceased were close friends. But that's not my responsibility. I'd suggest you warn the ladies to expect a stranger to be handling this investigation. Also myself and Constable Forbes will likely be conducting a search of the house and grounds, which may add to the distress, I'm afraid.'

'Of course, sir.'

Hardy walked to the hall door. Mr Roberts followed him. Hardy allowed the butler to precede him, then came out and shut the door, saying, 'I want this door locked until the local police, the police doctor, and the photographer arrive. Also, make sure no one, but no one, touches the garden door inside or out, or goes into the room from that side or this. Nothing is to be touched or removed without my authorisation, or that of any local investigating officer. Is that understood?'

'Yes sir, crystal clear. I'll see to it myself.'

'Thank you. And now, I'm afraid I will have to speak with Mrs Denholme.'

The butler gave him a worried look.

'What is it?' Hardy asked.

'Well, I'm afraid the doctor was called to Mrs Denholme. She was, as I'm sure you'd expect, very distressed. He's given her a sedative.'

Hardy sighed. 'Yes, I suppose that is understandable. Very well, I'll speak to the maid instead.'

Dottie had a sense of being haunted. It was nothing she could put her finger on, just a vague sensation that unsettled her, like a finger prodding her in the back. She had slept fairly well, apart from once or twice noticing the sound of a cockerel somewhere nearby, and the exasperated groans and grumbles from the room next door. She tried to analyse her reasons for feeling so odd, but it was impossible to pinpoint exactly what was irking her. She felt as though she'd seen or heard something that was insistent upon being recognised or acknowledged in some way. Her eye was continually drawn to the connecting door to the room next to hers. She checked for the third time that the door on her side was still locked.

She shook her head and gave up the attempt. She was fussing for no reason. She finished dusting powder over her shiny nose, and satisfied that the fault had been corrected, she went downstairs to her first breakfast at the inn.

There was only one table. Dottie had fondly pictured herself seated at a little white-linened table, gleaming cutlery gently carrying perfectly cooked eggs and bacon to her mouth. She had imagined a lovely hot little teapot and a dainty cup.

The reality was rather different. The little room that served guests as parlour, dining room, and as breakfast room too, contained one large oak table, heavy and dark, surrounded by a regiment of heavy wooden chairs. A miscellany of mismatched knives, forks and spoons lay in a heap in the table's centre.

The room's other occupants comprised a stout old woman and an even more obese, loudly panting Pekinese. The two of them were making rapid progress through a plate of kippers, a trail of butter and kipper-juice dotting the none-too-clean surface of the table from the woman's plate to the mouth of the hopeful dog, as it sat on the chair beside its mistress and yapped when it was ready for more.

Dottie couldn't help wrinkling her nose in distaste, though she quickly found a smile when the woman looked in her direction. This was the woman she'd seen going along the road last night, she realised, doubtless giving her dog a last walk before bedtime.

'Good morning,' Dottie said, repressing a shudder as the dog strained to lick drips from the tabletop.

All she got in return was a grunt. This might be enough to discourage most others, but Dottie was a persistent fellow-guest.

'Isn't it lovely to see the sun shining this morning? Quite a change after the weather we've been having lately.'

The woman stared at Dottie. The dog yapped and nudged the woman's arm with its nose, leaving an unsightly smudge on her sleeve. Dottie sighed, the exhalation sending her hair bouncing on her forehead. As she struggled to think of another comment to make, the door opened and a small, grey-haired woman wrapped in a faded housecoat bustled in and slapped a plate of kippers in front of Dottie.

'Oh, er...' said Dottie, surprised. Finally she added a slightly belated, 'Thank you.'

The woman gave Dottie a glare then turned on her heel and left.

'Gosh,' Dottie said, and she sent a rueful smile at the woman with the dog. Dottie looked down at her plate. The kippers swam figuratively if not literally in copious amounts of a buttery juice that was cooling and congealing rapidly. Her stomach seemed to contract in protest. A wave of nausea rose through her as the odour of the fish reached her nostrils. She pushed the plate away, and turned to the other woman.

'I don't suppose you'd like another couple of...'

She got no further. The plate was whisked away, denuded of its contents and the empty plate returned to Dottie within a matter of seconds.

'Don't mind if I do. Waste not, want not, I was always told. You won't mind if I give a few crumbs to Madame Bovary, I suppose?'

The dog, already salivating, yapped vigorously at the sound of its name. Doggy fishy breath engulfed Dottie. She shuddered and turned away, and with her handkerchief clamped over her nose and mouth, she managed to say, in a slightly muffled voice, 'Please do, I'm sure kippers are excellent for a dog's health. I do like her name, by the way.'

'My favourite book as a girl. Although my mother considered it most unsuitable for a young lady to read, of course. But I told her we were living in a modern world, and that I should contrive to read it in secret if she forbade my governess to give me a copy.'

'Ah, er,' said Dottie, unable to think of an intelligent response. But she was spared the need for further comment as the door was flung open and the landlady came in to deposit a fat brown china teapot in the middle of the table amongst the cutlery, then added two cups. 'Tea,' she said, and she turned to depart. Before she could do so, however, the elderly lady said, rather loudly,

'Hey! Just a minute! I'd like a pot of good strong coffee, please, and the same for this lady. With what we're paying for this place, you'd think we could at least get a choice of beverages. I certainly don't want any of this dishwater you call tea.'

The landlady looked at her with loathing, but said nothing, though she slammed the door with rather more force than necessary.

'Do you think she will?' Dottie asked. 'Bring us coffee, I mean?'

'Oh yes. It's our little daily ritual. Every day she brings in a pot of tea, weak as dishwater, and every day I tell her to take the muck away and bring me coffee. Don't be fooled by her appearance of surly unhelpfulness. She really is genuinely surly and unhelpful. Just like her brother who owns The Dirk, the other public house across the way. But, bless the woman, her husband gives her no help at all with this place, so she has to do everything. All he does all day is jaw with his friends and polish the odd beer glass. He spends the whole day behind that bar, even if it's outside licensing hours. Then there's a son, too.'

'Oh yes, Alex,' Dottie said. 'I met him last night, a

sweet boy.'

'Takes after his father. A layabout. Out until all hours with his chums, getting into trouble and making his mother's life a misery. Between him and his father, they've got all the useful qualities of my grandmother's aspidistra.'

Dottie was fascinated by the woman's manner of expressing herself. She held out her hand, somehow sure the woman would approve of shaking hands in the modern manner, like a man. She was right. The woman gripped Dottie's tiny hand in a cold but firm grip.

'I'm Dottie Manderson,' said Dottie. 'Just here for a few days.'

'Millicent Masters. Ditto.'

'Millicent... The Millicent Masters? The Half A Man Lay Dead Millicent Masters? Good heavens, but I adored that book! And your others, of course.'

'Your mother allows you to read them, then?' Miss Masters asked slyly.

'Er, well no,' Dottie was forced to admit. 'I read them in secret. My maid gets them for me.'

Miss Masters laughed heartily. 'That's priceless! A very gentile rebellion!'

The coffee appeared at that moment, accompanied by some lukewarm, lumpy porridge.

Dottie poked at the porridge with reluctance and ate a spoonful or two before pushing it away. She put sugar into her coffee to compensate for the lack of calories in her meal.

'So why are you here, of all places. Miss Dottie? It's not exactly the usual spot for tourists. Nor is it the perfect spot for early sun, picturesque enough for a secret love affair or remote enough for a rest cure.'

Dottie wasn't sure how much she should say, so she contented herself with a simple, 'I'm here to find someone.'

'Oh? Most enigmatic. May one enquire whom?'

'I don't know exactly. I'm to wait for information. Someone is going to contact me this afternoon.'

'More and more intriguing! Just like a spy novel.' Miss Masters broke off to appease a loudly yapping Madame Bovary with the last tiny morsels of kipper. Dottie had to turn away from the gruesome spectacle of the dog licking the table again, smearing fishy butter all over the oak surface.

Dottie wondered if Miss Masters was in fact the contact Mr Bray had told her to look out for. It seemed odd to find her in this out of the way place. Something particular had to have brought her here.

She said, 'I might ask you the same, Miss Masters. This is hardly one of the intellectual salons of Paris and the fin-de-siècle. I wouldn't have expected there to be any appeal to an author. Neither is it likely to encourage diligence, research opportunities, provide material, nor is the location one of a natural beauty calculated to inspire.'

'Ah,' said Miss Masters with a hard look. 'Very sharp of you.' She set her cup down in its saucer rather heavily. 'Between you and I, I'm here to keep an eye on someone. Even authors can be wives and mothers, you know. And now, if you'll excuse me, Madame Bovary needs her exercise. Have a nice day, as our American cousins say.'

Dottie was perusing the buttons on offer in the needlework shop in the village. The woman behind the counter, bored with her own company, was pleasantly surprised to have a lady from London in her shop, very eager to enter into conversation with her.

During the course of just two minutes she

discovered that, a) Dottie was staying at The Thistle, b) that she was visiting the area for a few days, c) that she didn't know anyone locally, d) that she was a keen knitter, e) that she required small buttons to finish off a matinee jacket for her elder sister's first baby, expected in the summer, f) that she was not herself married or courting—although, the shop woman told herself, she definitely had that look, there was a young man in the picture somewhere, of that she was certain—and finally, g) the young lady seemed prepared to spend a decent amount of money in return for good-quality local gossip.

In return, Dottie learned that the needlecraft shop was owned outright, as a gift from a previous laird to the former incumbent who had saved the laird's small son from the path of a careering horse. Apart from The Dirk, the rest of the village was owned by the laird, who was universally despised.

This mention of the laird led to a lengthy discussion of the shocking crime that occurred during the night.

'Dead as a doornail, right there in his study,' the shop-owner said with relish, and went on to furnish several more details that may or may not have been true.

Dottie discovered that the laird was a recent incomer with a talent for finding fault in everything and everyone. He had been married to a 'poor wee thing' who always looked as if she were on the point of tears. It seemed to be universally understood that the woman had to stand between her husband's bullying ways and their two small boys.

'Kept her practically under lock and key too. And it was common knowledge they owed every tradesmen in the area. Not that they lived lavishly. No dinner parties, no outings. No visits, no tea with the local big-wigs. So I've no idea what he could have spent his money on. Admittedly he played golf. And went out shooting or fishing. She stayed at home and cared for the children and did the flowers, and never a body to take tea with or anything. The dear Lord knows how long it's been since her own mother was shown the door. Just the first Christmas, her mother was there, then an almighty row, and never invited back. She wasn't even allowed to write to her.'

'I expect she managed somehow. I know I should,' Dottie said.

The shopkeeper nodded sagely.

'Aye, you and me both. But I don't see young Mrs Denholme having the courage, somehow. Well, they had to call the doctor to come out to give her something to make her sleep, this morning when her husband's body was discovered. The doctor was outside ma house at six o'clock, on his way back from seeing her, talking to the minister about it. But in time, she'll get over it, and at least now she'll be free of his cruel ways, and no doubt her eldest boy will grow up to be laird in his father's place, and a much finer job of it he'll make, I'm sure.'

'Oh dear, what a dreadful situation. To lose one's husband in such a violent manner.' Dottie pushed away one set of tiny pearl buttons, and took up another, very similar set. 'Although husbands are so difficult to please, sometimes, or so my sister tells me.'

'Aye, weel, some more than others, I'd say.'

Dottie agreed.

Changing the subject, the other woman went on to tell Dottie about the feud between the members of the McHugh family. The 'other' pub, The Dirk, had been left to a brother of the innkeeper's wife. 'And he'd walked out the house at fifteen years of age, and told them all to go to hell, right there in front of the minister. That was thirty years ago. Never heard of again until a year ago when the father died, though he was in Glasgow all along, apparently.'

Dottie reached for a couple of cotton reels to consider the colour of the thread against her matinee jacket. The shopkeeper continued.

'And then there was the daughter o' the family, spent years nursing the parents both to their graves. Then she found The Dirk had been left to this brother, right out from under her, the place where she'd lived her whole life up to that point.'

'Shocking,' said Dottie.

'Small wonder she and her husband took over The Thistle inn when the old landlord retired. Now they run it in competition with her brother, and the village men spend half their time in the one, and half in the other, to try and keep the peace.'

'Small wonder, indeed,' Dottie agreed.

'And that McHugh, he's another one who's a terrible bully. Always a-beating his new young wife, and a-calling her vile names. She's another poor stick. Though everyone knows she's back carrying on with that young rogue, aye, and that'll end in tears too. He may be easy on the eye, that one, but he's such an awful one for getting into trouble. Aye, I'm happier as a spinster.' But her wistful sigh said otherwise.

Dottie paid for her purchases and left after a few minutes' more conversation, this time only about the weather.

It never failed to intrigue her that everywhere—in the big, anonymous cities, and in the tiny country hamlets and villages—there lurked the same tempers, ambitions, hopes and resentments. Humans, it seemed, were the same wherever one found them.

It was mid-afternoon, and Hardy was with the procurator fiscal. It was fair to say that the two men did not see eye to eye. The procurator fiscal had pulled rank, and the inspector from London had been well and truly put in his place, and told to remove himself from the investigation. Hardy felt he had to try one last time to get his way.

'Sir, with respect, the scientific evidence from the crime scene does not bear out your suspicion that the crime was committed by an intruder from outside. This is a common wish in a small community, but a completely false one. I am certain we should be looking closer to home.'

The procurator was equally determined to prove his own viewpoint. 'But of course the evidence supports my suspicions! The footprints coming in from the garden, the use of the weapon, the threats, the thefts, the vandalism. It all points towards one local man who is known to have had a grudge against Denholme, who has a string of criminal convictions to his name, who was released from prison mere days before the crime took place, who has previously been convicted of poaching from the dead man's estate. And who had been seen in the area only an hour before the shooting. I suggest you return to London, Inspector, your assistance is no longer required. In any case, you are out of your area of authority. I do not want to hear of you involving yourself in matters that do not concern you. The Edinburgh police, are I assure you, the equal of Scotland Yard.'

'Of course, sir. But what about the muddy boots in the victim's dressing room? There was fresh mud on the heel of one and caught in the tread of the other. The same boots that made the footprints on the study floor. How did the dead man manage to get his boots freshly muddy? And none of the staff I interviewed had seen anyone, much less this man you mention, in the area during the whole of the evening. Or indeed, that entire day. And what about this missing letter?'

'Are you calling me a liar, Inspector?' the procurator asked through gritted teeth. 'The man's room had been ransacked, the safe opened and its contents gone, the desk drawers broken and emptied out onto the floor. And why shouldn't a man burn a letter in his own study, if he so wishes, pray? Who's to say that is in any way something sinister? Do you think I'm an idiot, Inspector?'

Hardy took a hold on his temper, surprised by the man's anger and defensiveness, not to mention how detailed his information was. 'No, sir, of course not. But I just feel...'

'Well you can take your feelings and get on back to London. We deal in facts and evidence up here, laddie, not feelings. And allow me to remind you, Hardy, the warrant I granted was for local law enforcement, not for outsiders to use as an excuse to poke about and upset innocent people. You are dismissed from the case, inspector, and that's an end to it. Now if you don't mind, I have things to do, including a visit to offer my condolences to poor wee Mrs Denholme.'

Hardy had no choice but to leave. He knew the procurator was correct about the warrant, although it hadn't actually been Hardy but Constable Forbes who had carried out the search, along with a part-time constable he had drafted in from Dunbar. As the only senior officer on the spot at that time, Hardy took the blame, for he certainly was out of his jurisdiction. Technically though, the search had been carried out by local officers, but he should have waited for an inspector to come out from Edinburgh. Even though no officers could be spared until the following morning due to their own pressing workload. Hardy felt he had done the only thing he could do, but the procurator saw it differently.

Unsure what else to do, Hardy drove back to Constable Forbes's house. The constable was in, as always, and at liberty to drink tea. Carefully, Hardy related the outcome of his conversation with the procurator. He tried to summarise the points dispassionately, unsure where the constable's allegiance might lie.

'Get that down you, laddie,' Forbes said, handing over the tea. 'Yon procurator's a fool, if you ask me. But of course, what would ye expect? Only been in the job a year. Promoted from some law firm in Edinburgh.'

'The victim was clearly his good friend. In spite of what the procurator says, I'm sure they were far more than just occasional golfing partners. He knew Mrs Denholme was small in stature, and of a nervous disposition. He described her as 'poor wee Mrs Denholme'. I feel he knows the woman personally.'

'Aye, man. It wasn't just the victim who was his good friend; the procurator was at school with Mrs Denholme's brother. He's known the whole family for years.'

'But then why is he so keen to see this local villain arrested for the shooting on so little evidence? I'd have thought he'd want a thorough investigation and the truth at all costs, if Mr Denholme and her family really are such good friends.'

'Aye, you'd think so. Though yon Hardy has been a thorn in the procurator's side for a while now.'

That name again. He found it irksome to hear it. It unsettled him, though that was ridiculous. Just

because some fellow had the same name as himself...
He reminded himself yet again that it wasn't the
most unusual of names. That it meant nothing.

After a second cup of tea, Hardy went to speak
with the late Mr Denholme's butler again. The butler
confirmed what he'd told Hardy previously. He'd
seen no one in or around the house at all during the
evening before the murder had taken place.

'Not even during the day,' Roberts said. 'Very
quiet it was yesterday and the day before. You're the
only visitor we've seen in almost a week.'

Just to make doubly sure, he spoke once again to
Mrs Roberts and the young maid, but they too said
the same. They were adamant. He believed them, yet
there was something odd, something he couldn't
quite pinpoint. They knew something that could help
him, he was certain. But how could he find out what
it was?

He asked to see Mrs Denholme, if she was free.
He half-expected her to point out that her good
friend the procurator had told her Hardy was off the
case, but she said no such thing. She stood in the
doorway, pale and anxious, clutching her hands
tightly in front of her and asked whether he would
like tea. He said yes please, gently and politely. She
rang, and asked the maid for the tea, then took a
seat, her hand trembling slightly as she smoothed her
skirt to sit. Had her husband made her this nervous,
Hardy wondered, or did she have a guilty conscience.

He asked her how she was feeling and extended
his condolences. She accepted them with a slight
inclination of the head, and told him she was feeling
a little better.

'The shock, you know.'

'Of course, Mrs Denholme. I can't imagine what
you must be going through. And your sons too, of

course.'

The tea arrived just as he was about to ask a question. He kept it back until she had finished the ritual of serving a cup of tea. Then:

'May I ask, Mrs Denholme, whether you heard anything out of the ordinary during the night?'

'A shot, do you mean?'

'Anything at all.'

She appeared to be thinking, though he wasn't convinced by her acting. She furrowed her brow and slowly shook her head. 'Nooo, sorry, I can't say I remember... But of course, I took a sleeping pill. I usually do, I don't sleep very well.'

'I see. And what time did you retire for the night?'

'At about ten o'clock.'

'And you took your sleeping pill right away, or later on, when you found you couldn't sleep?'

'Oh right away. They act very quickly too. I would have been asleep within five minutes or so.'

Privately he thought the pills didn't sound safe to take regularly if they were that strong, but outwardly he simply smiled and nodded. 'Of course. Thank you. And then the doctor came, in the morning, and gave you something for the shock, I understand?'

She smiled, and appeared quite relaxed as she said, 'Oh yes, that's right, Inspector.'

'And what time was that, please?'

The smile faded. He thought she was trying to decide on an appropriate time.

She said, 'I believe it was just about seven o'clock.'

'How long had you been awake?'

'Not very long. Perhaps twenty minutes or so. I was awakened by the commotion downstairs.'

He nodded again, thinking it sounded a bit tight, time-wise. 'The discovery of your husband's body? I suppose the maid screamed?'

'Er, well, I don't actually know. She may have done. All I know is that something woke me.'

'Had you seen anyone hanging about the place in recent weeks?'

She shook her head.

'And had your husband received any threats or had any disagreements lately?'

Again she shook her head, but added, 'I'm afraid I know very little about my husband's business arrangements, however.'

'I see, thank you.' He took up his teacup and drank a little tea. They talked for a few minutes of dogs, and children and the difficulties of finding the right school. Ten minutes of that, and he said goodbye to her, thanking her with genuine gratitude for the tea.

She relaxed, clearly relieved it was all over.

It didn't make sense, Hardy thought as he returned to the village. Was there any way things could have got muddled because he had been to see Mr Denholme? Were the procurator's wires getting crossed because of the similarity in name between himself and this local villain?

In the village, he asked again. He went to The Thistle and asked there if anyone had seen the 'other' William Hardy, or knew where he could be found. No one could tell him anything. He went to the general store, the manse, the needlework shop, and even—at great risk to himself—to The Dirk, and asked if anyone had seen local man William Hardy in or around the grounds of the laird's house at any time on the night he was murdered, or in fact anywhere in the locality. No one had seen him. Surely the procurator was wrong. Who were these witnesses who claimed that they had seen the man?

He decided to go back to the bar of the inn and see if he could get some tea. He felt as though he was just going over and over the same ground and getting nowhere. He needed to think. If only he had Sergeant Maple here to help him. It was always useful to have someone to talk his ideas through with, and he missed Maple's good sense and even better humour.

As walked across the road, he heard someone call out, 'Inspector!'

Turning, Hardy found himself looking into a mirror. Or so he thought at first. Then he realised it was another person, the very image of himself. He was speechless. The man laughed at his surprise, then holding out his hand, he said, 'I hear you've been asking after me. Allow me to introduce maself. I'm William Hardy.'

The William Hardy who came from London had nothing to say. He continued to stare, not taking the other man's hand. The other man dropped his hand back by his side, affronted, and said, 'I was going to say, I hear you've been using ma name, but now you're right in front of me, I can see it's no just ma name you're using, but ma face too. Though I generally take better care of mine.'

The two men faced each other. William still had no idea what to say. He felt as if he'd been punched in the gut. There was no longer any point in rationalising—the evidence spoke overwhelmingly. This was no mere coincidence of name. He had another brother. An older brother. One with his face, his stature and even—how could that be—his name. He stared.

The other man stared back, his aggression seeping away. William Hardy of Lower Bar shook his head. 'I don't understand...'

'Unfortunately, I believe I understand all too well,' William Hardy of London said. Rage began to fill his whole being, and turning abruptly, he marched away in the direction of The Thistle.

Fighting his desire to punch something or someone, he headed up the stairs to his room. He would splash some cold water on his face—carefully—then sit in his room for a while. That would give him the chance to calm down and think rationally.

Rounding the top of the stairs, in the imperfectly lit upper hall, he walked straight into her. They bumped, they leapt back in surprise, polite apologies on both their lips. Then:

'William!' said Dottie, astonished, whilst at the same time he said, rather less politely,

'What the hell!'

His words died on his lips. Joy at the sight of her flooded him. He smiled, then seizing her in a crushing bearhug, he said her name softly against her hair. Then good manners broke out between them, reminding them they were in a public albeit quiet place. They each took a step back. Dottie patted her hair, William pushed his hands into his pockets.

'What on earth happened to your face? Have you been in a brawl?' Dottie asked, leaning to peer more closely at his right eye and cheekbone. The nose, still rather red, was now mercifully almost its normal size again. He realised that no one had yet hit him today, although he had a feeling it had come fairly close more than once.

'What this? Oh yes, something like that. Does it look awful?' Dammit, he thought, I'd forgotten about the black eye. And the bruise. He felt embarrassed. He felt overwhelmed by the events of the last day or two. He wanted to be with her, but had an irresistible urge to get away by himself for a few minutes. He hesitated.

'It is rather purple and noticeable. Does it hurt?' She looked concerned.

'Just a bit.' He couldn't help sounding a little snappy.

'Oh dear, sorry. Let's talk about something else. Er—when did you arrive?'

'The night before last,' he said. 'And you?'

'Yesterday.'

'I wish I'd known you were going to be here...'

'Mr Bray asked me not to say anything about where I was going.' She bit her lip, and added, 'Sorry. I didn't feel I could disobey him, he was so sweet to me. I didn't dare let him down.' She thought for a moment then added further, 'I was told to meet someone here, and that person would tell me how I could fulfil my errand. But no one's turned up. They were supposed to contact me this afternoon. But... What were you doing at Mr Bray's office the other day? Are you my contact?'

He could only nod. So many things were falling into place. Old Bray had sent him up here, had wanted him to meet the other... He couldn't call him his brother. Would never call him that.

Dottie was saying, 'Sorry I didn't let you know. Although you didn't say anything either, so...'

His mouth twisted in an apology. 'No. Mr Bray also told me not to...'

'Ah.'

It was ridiculous, she thought. They were standing in the inn's hallway, and neither of them seemed able to think of a single intelligent thing to say. But just as she was wracking her brains, he said suddenly, 'Have you had dinner?'

'Oh no, not yet.'

'I know it's a bit early, but would you like to have dinner with me? Unless of course...'

'That would be lovely, William, I'd like that.' She attempted a smile. It felt stiff and awkward on her face. What on earth was the matter with her? Usually she had no end of smart small-talk to ease along any situation. But she was talking to him as if they were virtual strangers, stumbling and fumbling for banalities.

He hesitated for a moment, then said, 'Shall we say half an hour? I need to have a quick bath and get changed. There's a little place in Dunbar that does good food.'

'How will we...?'

'Oh, I've rented a car.'

'Of course,' she nodded. And her social skills finally failing her completely, she turned and went back to her room without another word, whilst in her head berating herself furiously for being an idiot.

In her room, she shut the door with a sense of relief and leaned against it, her eyes shut. A cool breeze from the nearby window fanned her hot face, helping her to compose herself.

There was the sound of a key turning in a lock so close at hand that for a moment she thought he had entered her room. A door shut, and she realised it was him—he was the one in the room right next door. There was a creak of bed springs followed soon by two soft thumps as he kicked off his boots onto the carpet. She heard him clear his throat in what she thought of as his own characteristic manner.

It seemed obvious now. She realised she must have heard him do exactly that, that very morning in the early hours, and subconsciously she had recognised the sound, had known his voice. That was why she felt so haunted, so edgy. The sense of his nearness had scratched at her memory all day. Oh, it was all too close.

She hurried over to the window. After a moment she turned and looked at the connecting door. What would he do, she wondered, if she were to open the connecting door and go into his room? She smiled ruefully to herself. She knew exactly what would happen. For a full minute she debated with herself whether she had the courage to actually do what she wanted to do. But then she thought of her mother and father, her sister and all their friends and family, and realised she could never, ever risk putting herself in such a position that the very mention of her name would be a scandal.

She heard him go along the corridor, and judged that he had gone for his bath. Out of pure curiosity, she checked the connecting door. It was locked on her side. With a delicious sense of doing something very naughty, she unlocked her side, opened it and found another door directly behind it, as she had known she would. She tried the second door. It opened.

That rather surprised her. She went into his empty room, and drifted about. His suitcase—which had certainly seen better days—was sitting open on the chest of drawers. She browsed. Right on top was a large brown envelope. She recognised Mr Bray's handwriting on the front. The envelope wasn't sealed. She took a quick peek. The first thing she saw was the large quantity of banknotes. Her curiosity intensified. There was another, small envelope and a few other bits of paper, reservations and other travel details. It was all very interesting.

What was William up to? Had he really come all this way just to tell her his half of the secret—the location of Mrs Carmichael's son?

Also in the suitcase were two shirts, one clearly new, the other somewhat frayed on the cuffs and the points of the collar. There was a warm sweater, handknitted, of course. She held it to her face and inhaled, but disappointingly it smelled only of the laundry. There were a couple of pairs of socks rolled up, and on examination these proved to have a hole in either the toe or heel of all four socks. The underwear, rendered a dreary grey by too many washings, she pushed aside hastily, her face hot with embarrassment. There was a tie in the colours of his old school. There were two handkerchiefs, one with his initials in the corner, and it was of good quality stuff but again, rather aged, and fraying at the corners. It was clearly a throwback to an earlier, wealthier time. She closed the lid of the suitcase down and saw the peeling label:

Master William Hardy,
Repton School,
Etwall,
Derbyshire.

It came as no surprise that he'd had the suitcase for so long, probably fifteen, even twenty years. Her heart wanted to weep for the little boy sent away to boarding school at so young an age, as most little boys of their class seemed to be. How grateful she was that she and Flora had been day-girls for the entirety of their education. Not once had she wished to stay at school at the end of the day. As young as she was back then, she had known she was lucky to go home to her family each evening.

His wallet lay on the bed beside the ordinary metal comb, a small penknife with a mother-of-pearl handle, yet another folded handkerchief, and a wristwatch. It struck her that she'd never seen him wearing a watch. Did he keep it in his pocket? Or was she just horribly unobservant? She wasn't sure. It was an ordinary watch with a good plain dial and a supple leather strap. The underside of the strap was worn smooth and soft, perhaps from lying against his skin for a number of years.

Apart from these things, and his overcoat hanging on the back of the door, that was all he had with him. Were there no pyjamas? She checked the suitcase again including, this time, the pile of underwear—certainly in need of replacing—and she even looked underneath the pillow but could find none. So, what on earth did he wear in bed, she wondered. Then the very obvious answer hit her, and she flushed with embarrassment once more, and had to have a stern word with her imagination which had already begun to furnish her with pictures. She shook her head. She was as bad as a man—seemingly with a one-track mind!

Now she felt the weight of time on her. Had she been in his room for five minutes or twenty? She couldn't be sure, but to be safe, she hurried back through the connecting door and shut it firmly behind her, turning the key in the lock on her side.

She sat in front of the mirror, tutted at the sight of her flushed face and guilty expression, and set to work with her cosmetics, hoping to goodness that by the time they left the hotel, she would have lost that wild, speculative look in her eye.

Hardy returned from his bath and shave just a few minutes later. He was feeling calmer, though still on edge. He couldn't get that face out of his head. Clearly he would have to have a further conversation with the other William Hardy, but he wanted nothing to do with the man. As far as he was concerned, the fellow could go to hell.

As soon as he stepped into his room, he was aware of her scent. Dottie had been in here. He wondered briefly how she had got in, then he noticed the connecting door and thought, with a grin, of course. A riot of ideas flooded his mind.

Dumping his wash-bag and towel on the chair, he crossed to the door and oh-so-carefully eased open his side, then bent to examine hers to see if the door was locked, all the time keen to make no noise at all. He heard the sound of her door to the hall open and close, and heard the key turned in the lock. Her soft footsteps went along the corridor to the bathroom.

Making the most of the opportunity, he turned the handle to her door. It was locked. He could see the key in the lock. It took approximately twenty seconds for him to get his penknife and push the key out onto the waiting sheet of newspaper he'd pushed under the door, as demonstrated in all the best boys' adventure stories, and thus he gained access to her room. He hadn't time to look around, and in any case, felt it would be an unpardonable breach of etiquette. So he did the only thing he could think of, taking another twenty seconds, then he turned her key in the lock once more, slipping the key under the door.

He went back to his room. He dressed in clean clothes and combed his hair. He liked the neat way she had folded everything in his suitcase—clearly her conscience had been untroubled by the etiquette that had held him back—and it was all so much neater than he'd accomplished.

He heard someone enter the room next door, and just a moment later heard her muffled exclamation. He smiled.

As he knocked on her door a few minutes later, he felt happy, his spirits soaring, though he was a little nervous of his reception if she hadn't taken his little joke in good part.

She opened the door, hand on hip and gave him a schoolma'am look of amused exasperation. His watch hung from one slender fingertip, her nail through the buckle.

'I believe this is yours?'

He feigned surprise. 'Oh yes, so it is. I'd wondered where I'd left that. I've been looking everywhere...' Giving her a roguish grin, he took it and put it in his pocket.

'Well, just so you know, now that I'm aware you can get into my room even if the door is locked, I've put the chair-back under the handle.'

'You started it,' he said, but with a smile. 'Now then, dinner?'

'Yes please, William.' She swept past him haughtily, her head held high, though this was somewhat spoiled by her having to dash back and lock her door.

They spoke little on the drive. Dottie relaxed against the leather seat and enjoyed the scenery parading past the window, bathed in the deep golden glow that comes just before twilight. Why did the sun only shine for the last half-hour before the end of the day?

When he parked the car, he got out and came round to open her door for her. She thanked him for the courtesy, old-fashioned now, but nonetheless welcome. He held his hand out to help her step down.

'Mind the puddles.'

She almost said, we sound just like an old married couple, but couldn't quite bring herself to say those words. She was aware of her silence, but felt a new constraint in his company. She felt shy. She couldn't think of anything to say. But William, too, seemed distracted and deep in thought. Perhaps the murder case was on his mind?

The 'restaurant' she had imagined, turned out to be a fried fish stall next to the beach. William gave their orders to the smiling woman behind the counter, and when the food was handed over, wrapped in newspaper of course, they ate it as they walked by the water, along with a number of other 'diners': lovers, young and old, families with gambolling children, solitary people, and groups of laughing friends.

They turned to walk beside the ancient ruins of the castle walls, then turned back once more to look at the little crowd of boats moored for the night. Then they returned to the beach. It was almost dark now, and they had finished their food long ago. William disposed of the papers in a waste bin. Dottie licked her fingers then wiped them carefully on her little handkerchief.

A noisy family vacated a bench, William swooped in to claim it, and Dottie joined him. The sun was a smudge of orange on the horizon. They watched until it disappeared completely, seemingly beneath the sea. All about them was navy blue sky with glittering stars, and the murmur of gentle waves. A breeze came in off the sea, chilly enough to warrant William's arm about her shoulders, holding her against the warmth of his body.

Conversation was still infrequent, but Dottie felt a deep contentment. Surely this feeling of gentle happiness was love? Over the centuries, so much had been written, spoken, and sung about love, but did anyone really know what it was?

Here and there a lamp glowed into life, casting a small patch of gold onto the ground, adding to the romantic timelessness of the evening. After a while, they walked again. Dottie decided to risk Mr Bray's wrath and tell William everything. The other promenaders had gone, leaving behind only a few shy lovers and dog-walkers.

As soon as she had told him, he halted in his tracks.

'Mrs Carmichael had a child,' he repeated. His head was spinning with the thoughts that rushed in on him. He shook his head as he saw the truth now for the first time. He should have seen it sooner. He had known all along, he realised. Of course, this wasn't just about who the father was, but the mother too. And oh yes, he had known, somehow...

Dottie, disappointed by his lack of surprise, continued, unaware of the turmoil in him. 'Yes, and apart from the fact that it was a baby boy, I don't know any more. She had to give him up for adoption, of course. I don't have much of an idea how to go about finding him. I was supposed to be hearing from someone who can help me this afternoon, but no one has got in contact. I imagine there's still time, though. After all, I only arrived yesterday. All the same, I can't help wishing I had more to go on.'

'Hmm,' he said. He looked about him, hesitating. 'Do you mind if we go back now? I—er—it's been rather a long day.'

'Of course,' she said. In her mind she was wondering what she had said to upset him. His mood had changed instantaneously from light-hearted and romantic to withdrawn and taciturn. She berated herself, then had to hurry to catch him up.

'William!'

'What?' he asked, then caught himself. He took a

breath. 'I'm sorry, Dottie. Do forgive me, I didn't mean to snap.'

She lay a hand on his arm. 'What is it? What have I done?' Her voice was small, uncertain, a child's voice.

'Nothing, dear, nothing. It's not you.' He patted her hand, but his mood persisted, and when he left her at the door of her room, his kiss on her cheek was perfunctory at best.

'Damn the man!' she said to herself crossly, but careful to keep her voice down, as she heard his door open and close, and the groan of his bedsprings.

*

Day Five: Saturday

Inspector Hardy was up very early on Saturday morning. At last he had slept better than the two previous nights, being so tired he had been completely unaware of the cockerel's announcements.

On his way out of the inn, he paused in the bar and spoke to Mr Nelson.

'Have there been any phone calls for me?'

Nelson shook his head. 'I'm sorry, sir, nothing.'

'I'm expecting a call from London. It's very important so if I'm not here, could you please ask them to contact Constable Forbes?' Nelson was already nodding his agreement. 'And please remember it's confidential police business, so don't mention anything you learn to anyone other than myself.'

Nelson assured him he would be the soul of discretion.

Hardy had breakfast with Constable Forbes in

what had become something of a routine between them.

'The inspector from Edinburgh said he would be here by lunchtime,' Forbes said.

Hardy nodded. 'I'll make myself scarce. But look, before that, I need to ask you a favour. I want to talk to the pathologist who is examining the body. Can you tell me who it's likely to be, and where to find the man?'

'More than that, I'll take ye there maself.'

Forbes got to his feet, grabbed his jacket and was getting into Hardy's car before Hardy had come out of the house.

Hardy introduced himself to the pathologist, and began to explain the peculiar nature of his involvement. The pathologist waved it all aside, with a simple, 'Nothing to do with me.'

Hardy smiled. 'I'd be very grateful if you'd let me know the salient points of the Denholme case.'

'Aye well, I had him on the table last night. My wife was not best pleased when I came home late. She had invited friends to us for dinner.'

Hardy nodded sympathetically. 'Not a career that considers the needs of a family man.'

'Aye, you can say that again. Let me get ma notes.' He went into a little office, calling to them to come with him. He took up a card folder from his desk, and flipped it open. 'D'ye want to read the whole thing, or...?'

Hardy shook his head.

Forbes was looking around him with great interest. 'Never been here before,' he said to Hardy in a hushed voice.

'If you ever make a move to CID, you'll be in here more often than your own parlour,' Hardy told him grimly.

'Here we are, gentlemen. No big surprises. Reasonable health for a man of forty-six. Killed by a shotgun wound to the abdomen, death instantaneous. Range, between ten and twelve feet at the most. The shot retrieved from the corpus indicates you are looking for the usual standard 12-bore. He'd been dead about eight or nine hours when I saw him. Which was, according to my notes, 8.25 in the morning.'

'Did you notice the position of the body?' Hardy asked.

'Hmm. The typical falling position, indicating the victim was standing when shot.'

'And so the approximate height of the attacker would be...?'

'Entirely your problem, Inspector.'

'Humour me, please. About five feet tall, would you say?'

'Probably a little below average height, unless they held the shotgun in some peculiarly theatrical way or knelt on the floor. Which seems unlikely. So a good guess would be about five feet tall, or thereabouts.'

Hardy, smiling for the first time that day, shook the pathologist's hand and said goodbye.

He drove himself and Forbes back to the village. As he got out of the car, he said to Forbes, 'Where will I find my namesake?'

Forbes stared at him. 'Your...? Oh, right. Hmm, well I dinna rightly know. He's usually a lot easier to find after dark. He'll either be sleeping off the booze somewhere, or chasing some skirt, or even, and this doesn't happen often, mind, working at one of the local farms. You'd have to drive all over the county to find him. Best let him come to you.'

That wasn't much help. Hardy said, 'Doesn't he have family in the area?'

'Oh no, he was adopted as a baby from some wealthy Englishwoman. Now I think of it, I think she was from London. Something to do with dressmaking, I think. His illegitimacy was never a secret, apart from whoever his father was, eh?' He gave Hardy a man-to-man nudge. 'He was brought up by an old couple who didn't have any little ones of their own. But they're both long gone, and the farm's had two or three tenants since then.'

Dottie had hoped to see William at breakfast, but he didn't appear. Not realising he'd gone out two hours earlier, she contemplated but dismissed the idea of knocking on his door with some invented excuse.

After forty minutes in the small dining parlour that reeked of kippers and Pekinese for the second morning, Dottie craved some fresh air. She excused herself and ran up to her room, grabbed her coat and hat, then ran back down again to hand in her key at the bar, fulfilling Mr Nelson's request that all guests hand in their keys if going out. No doubt it facilitated cleaning, Dottie thought, though surely they had a master key? Not that the inn appeared to be run along such commonsensical lines.

She stepped into the dimness of the bar, the smell of tobacco and stale beer catching in her throat. Surely not everywhere in Scotland was such an assault on the olefactory organs?

She was almost at the bar when she heard someone say his name. It stopped her in her tracks. A neat side-step took her behind a vast dusty aspidistra on a pedestal, and holding her breath, she eavesdropped without the slightest sense of shame.

'Only been here a few days, but twice he's already been caught 'at it' with Anna. Billy McHugh's ready to knock his block off, or worse, so if you see our dear Mr Hardy, tell him to watch his back.'

It was the voice of a man who'd just come in. Dottie had a feeling she'd seen him before. When he came back towards the door, she saw his uniform. Yes, it was the postman. He tipped his cap to Dottie who was now carefully examining a newspaper she'd found.

'Miss.'

She nodded and gave him an automatic smile, her mind replaying his words. The landlord, though, unaware of this minor side-play, was calling a merry rejoinder after the postman.

'Oh aye, I'll tell yon Master William to keep his trews on, not that telling'll make any difference to the man. He just can't leave that girl alone, husband or no. Good morning to ye.'

It was as much as she could bear. No longer caring what anyone thought, she pushed past the postman and out into the street, running headlong in the direction of the coast road, tears streaming down her face, sobs causing her breath to stumble. It couldn't, it just couldn't...

She halted. Frantically looking about her, she spied a tiny church nestling amongst rocks and trees on her right. She ran for the sparse cover of the trees, the heavens had just at that moment decided to open.

It couldn't be true. William Hardy? Surely he'd never...?

The graveyard had a calming effect on her stormy emotions. One hundred years from now, none of this will matter, she thought, mainly because she was surrounded by headstones which bore dates of the

1830s and 1840s. Not that this philosophical point helped her a jot. The heavy rain lightened to a soft shower. She stepped beneath the canopy of a large yew, though she was already quite wet. It was a shame there was no bench, as it was a pleasant spot. She leaned back against the rough bark and allowed the breeze and the patter of the raindrops to lull her mind, bringing her thoughts to peace.

After ten minutes, she began to feel there had to be a simple explanation. The William Hardy she knew would never carry on an intrigue with a married woman, let alone in such a... public... fashion. But did she know him?

The question was an answering whisper at the back of her mind. If she had given herself to him, that would have prevented him seeking solace elsewhere. Wouldn't it? Or would it? Was he, in fact, a womaniser? Just how well did she really know him? She shook herself impatiently. This was nonsense. If there was anything she was sure about with him—and she acknowledged she knew precious little—it was the unshakeable integrity of his character. She was wasting her tears for no reason. She was a little fool. It wasn't true, he would never do such a thing. She had nothing to worry about. He would never do any such thing.

Having reached this conclusion, she felt relieved. As if in answer to her lighter mood, the rain ceased and the sun came out from behind the veil of mist.

She emerged from under the yew tree, and began to look around, taking in the gentle beauty of the Victorian church and graveyard, and smiling at the rapid darts of blackbirds and squirrels.

Something rather larger than a squirrel bounded up to her, yapping joyfully and placing muddy paws on her skirt. A short distance away, Dottie noted with concern, a large quantity of earth had been heaped out onto the grassy path, not twelve inches from a tilting headstone.

'You naughty dog!' Dottie scolded the barking, wriggling creature, trying to wipe the mud from her clothes with her dainty hankie. 'You might be the same breed, but you're clearly not Madame Bovary, she's twice your size. So who are you?' She looked about but couldn't see anyone who appeared to be in charge of the dog. The Pekinese wore a collar, but there was no tag.

The back door of the church opened, and a woman in a flowered overall came out to empty a dustpan into a bin tucked away in a corner. She nodded and called 'Good morning!' to Dottie.

'I don't suppose you knew whose dog this is?' Dottie asked. The woman laughed.

'It looks like Gustave. He belongs to Mrs Denholme, up at the big house. Well, really I think it belongs to the boys, but they don't seem to do much with it other than throw the ball. They're not very good at keeping it under control, as you can see. It'll get run over one of these days, if they don't train it better.'

'Mrs Denholme?'

'Yes. Not that anyone will be paying much attention to the dog after what's happened.'

'Oh? Why is that?' Dottie already knew, of course, but was interested in finding out more.

The woman glanced quickly about her then came closer, dropping her voice. 'Why her husband, the laird, got himself shot dead the night before last. She'll be in deep mourning, of course, and the doctor was up there to give the poor woman some knock-out drops. Though from what I've heard, it couldnae be grief that took her so bad. Still, we mustn't speak ill o' the dead.'

Dottie resisted the urge to cry out, 'Oh please do', and instead responded with, 'Oh no, of course not.' Then feeling rather sly, she said, 'Though really, when a loved one passes away, those around them tend to forgive and forget the little niggles and foibles.'

The woman in the overall gave a knowing smile. 'I suppose so, if you can call a foul raging temper and a ready fist a little niggle. But, excuse me, Miss, I've got to get on.'

Dottie kept her long enough to find out where Mrs Denholme lived. She removed the belt from her dress. It was only there to show off her slim waist, in any case, it didn't serve any actual purpose. Looping the belt through the dog's collar as a makeshift lead, she set off, slowly due to the dog's enquiring nature, in the direction of the big house.

It wasn't hard to find, it being the only large house, or indeed house of any size, on this side of the church.

As she emerged from a copse of trees onto the edge of a vast expanse of lawn, Dottie spotted a couple of small boys playing with a ball. The dog yapped vigorously when it saw them, and the boys came running.

'I found your dog in the churchyard,' Dottie said. 'It is your dog, isn't it?'

'Golly!' said the first boy, aged about eight, Dottie judged.

'Was he digging up bones again?' the smaller one asked.

'I do hope not,' Dottie replied, though rather doubtfully, remembering the hole she'd seen. 'He's not very well trained, is he?'

'No. Father was always threatening to shoot him

if he didn't buck his ideas up.'

'At least we can keep him now!' the younger added. Neither child seemed particularly upset about the loss of their father, if indeed the dead man had been their father.

But the younger boy straight away said, his face flushed with excitement, 'Our father got shot to death yesterday!'

'Shush, Michael!' said his brother severely. 'Mama is very upset. She had to lie down, and the doctor had to be called.'

'I'm not surprised,' Dottie said, thinking that if her husband was ever shot dead, she'd require a bit more than a lie-down to recover from it. 'I'm sure everyone will expect you both to be on your best behaviour until your mama is feeling better.'

'I'm not upset,' the older boy told her. 'And neither's Michael.' He nudged his little brother.

'I am upset,' declared Michael, though his smiling, ruddy countenance said otherwise.

'At least now I don't have to go away to school,' the older boy said. 'Mama and I were both upset about that.'

'I'm not sure you should be telling me that,' Dottie said, just as Michael added,

'Lots of things will be better now Father isn't here.'

Dottie felt shocked. How very sad that a family should perceive the death of its head in such a way. To stem any further awkward revelations, she said briskly, 'Now boys, which is the way to the back door?' She had been unsure about whether she should simply leave or let someone know she had found the dog wandering, but decided it would be best to at least tell a staff member.

'This way,' Michael said, and to his brother, 'Race

you!' They charged off, the dog yapping at their heels, Dottie's belt trailing along the ground behind it. Dottie followed slowly, looking around her as she went.

A policeman stood guard at a pair of glass doors at the back of the house. One door stood open, and a photographer was taking pictures of it this way and that, no doubt trying to capture any prints or marks on the glass or frame.

'That's where it happened.' The older boy was by her side once more.

'Goodness,' said Dottie politely. She looked at the door with interest. The policeman stared at her as if defying her to come any closer. The younger boy came up to her and slipped his hand inside hers.

'This way, Ma'am,' he said, and for a moment Dottie was reminded of an adolescent boy by the name of Anthony whom she had met a few months earlier whilst engaged on a job for Mrs Carmichael. He too had shown a very adult sense of good manners. She hoped Anthony was all right.

They reached the back door and went inside without knocking. Dottie could hear a conversation going on. A man's voice was saying, 'Got lovely manners, has that London policeman. Shame he's not going to be in charge of the investigation.'

That must be William he's talking about, Dottie thought, with a sense of pride. Then she remembered the reason for her hasty departure from the inn that morning, and felt a momentary qualm. She pushed it down, telling herself yet again, no, William would never get involved with a married woman.

Another voice, female, responded with, 'Good looking too. Not that it's anything to do with it. I bet he doesn't miss much. I wouldn't mind him taking down my particulars, I can tell you.'

'You get on with those spuds, missy,' said the man's voice again, laughing. 'Anyway, they've pushed him out, haven't they? Procurator's orders.'

'No doubt afraid he'd get too close for comfort,' said a third voice, also female, and older-sounding, with something of a wheeze behind the Scottish accent.

Interesting, thought Dottie. She would have liked to hear more, but the boys raced in ahead of her to shout that there was a lady at the back door, and that she had found Gustave eating dead people in the graveyard.

The man said, 'That damned dog!' There was a scraping of a chair and he came out to find her hovering in the hallway.

'Pardon my French, Miss. I'm Roberts, the butler. Can I be of assistance?'

'Oh Mr Roberts. How do you do? I'm Dottie Manderson. I'm staying in the village for a few days. I'm sorry to disturb you all. I didn't want to go to the front door, as I had heard about the—er—tragedy. I just thought I ought to let someone know I found the dog wandering in the churchyard and thought I'd better bring him back. He—er—had been digging. Though I don't think he got as far as actually eating anyone,' she added with a smile.

Roberts pulled a face.

Michael shouted with relish, 'I bet he could smell the bones!'

Someone shushed him.

'Thank you so much Miss. I promise we'll try and keep a better eye on him. Er—I'm afraid I can't offer you any refreshment at the moment.'

Dottie backed away towards the door, a hand raised in apology. 'No, no. I quite understand, I don't want to intrude. Very distressing for you all, I'm sure.'

'I'm not distressed!' the older boy announced proudly.

'Well you should be, Master Jeffrey, now get along to the kitchen and Mrs Roberts will give you a glass of milk and some cherry cake.'

With a whoop of joy, the older boy ran off, the dog yapping at his heels once more. Dottie said goodbye and walked back to the churchyard. It was an hour later that she remembered her belt.

William Hardy needed to think. After leaving Forbes at the police house, he drove south then east until he reached the coast again. It was fortunate he saw little other traffic as his mind was barely focused on driving. He ranted to himself and thumped the steering wheel a couple of times.

At last he stopped the car by the strand where he had walked with Dottie the previous evening. It was deserted now yet bathed in as much golden sunshine as any fashionable pleasure-beach on the English Riviera.

He realised he was breathing hard, and made an effort to calm down. Leaning back in his seat, he closed his eyes and allowed the sound of the sea to wash over him. After a while his rage began to subside to a dull simmer.

Clearly, Mrs Carmichael's revelation to him at Dottie's tea-party two or three months earlier, had stopped some distance short of the truth.

I knew your father.

My God, he thought. His experience of life and the world, gained over time, and through his work in the police force, now furnished his mind with the untold details heard hundreds of times before. There had been an affair. That much he already knew, from

Mrs Carmichael's own lips, and confirmed by his uncle. The affair had been broken off when his father had met and married his mother, who was a more suitable match in terms of social class. According to his uncle, there was a resumption of the affair at some point and, as was now only too clear, in the midst of all this, a child had been conceived, and due to its illegitimacy had been put up for adoption, probably through informal channels, to spare everyone's feelings and reputations.

Hardy felt a disgust for the manners of his father's generation. To carry on like that, to produce a child and discard it, yet to preserve at all costs the outward façade of petty decency. He could hardly believe it. His antipathy towards his father had deepened into pure hatred over the last day or so, as first doubt, then suspicion, had crystallised into certainty and discovery.

He pulled out the watch that was in his pocket. It had been a last modest gift from his father. William had treasured it, had hoped some day to give it to his own son. Not that it was an expensive timepiece, nor one of any special craftsmanship, but his emotional attachment went far beyond its physical properties. William had left school and had gone up to Oxford to study law. He remembered his father, Major Garfield Hardy, shaking his hand as he and his wife readied themselves to leave on that first day. His father had handed him the tiny parcel, the box containing the watch.

'It's not much, William, I'm afraid. But it's practical. And not of sufficient value for you to get mugged for it, lose it in a card game, or pawn it to pay your bar bill. Just wear it and know your father is very proud of his son.'

Then they had shaken hands in the formal way

his father preferred, and William had kissed his mother, and they had gone, leaving him behind, in a strange place, among strange people, a young man on the brink of his adult life.

There had been a card in the box, a small pasteboard thing. His father's spidery script said, 'To my dear son William, with his father's love'. It was as close as they would ever get to an embrace. For the last ten years, he had treasured those few words, and all through the financial and personal disasters that came two short years after that day. He had treasured the words 'dear' and 'love', words never spoken aloud to him by his father yet always craved by his son.

Now, though, how much did those words really mean? Nothing. Less than nothing. Even his name wasn't his own. He shook his head in sheer disbelief. Even his name was not his own. By the time he had been born, his father already had another son called William Hardy. The watch could have been meant for either of them. To my dear son William. But which one?

He had an urge to fling it into the sea. He even got out of the car and went down to the eagerly lapping waves at the water's edge. He raised his hand, the watch there in his palm, and then... he couldn't do it.

With a sigh, he put the watch back in his pocket, angrily dashed away the tear on his face, winced at the pain from the bruise he rubbed by mistake, then he turned and went back to the car.

At the inn once more, in his room, he opened the big brown envelope and quickly found the smaller envelope inside. It contained the paper Mr Bray had given him to get signed by the 'missing heir'. Now he wanted to know what it said. He ripped the envelope open and pulled out the paper to read it. The paragraph was short but to the point:

I, William Garfield Hardy, do hereby swear and attest that I am the true son and blood relative of Muriel Carmichael and Garfield Edward Hardy, both deceased. By thus lawfully affirming my identity, I take control of the inheritance from my mother's estate.

Underneath there was a place for the signature, the date, and the signature of a witness.

William sank down on the bed. It was bad enough to give up his name to this man, but now he was to receive an inheritance too, whilst William was paid, in essence, a finders' fee of £500, and the rest of his siblings went without. This illegitimate son even had their father's name for his middle name. It wasn't... he shook his head again. All he could think was, it wasn't fair. He didn't care if it was childish, that was his only thought: that it wasn't fair.

Rage, cold and hard, knotted itself in the pit of his stomach.

She decided to go back for her belt after dinner. Hopefully then she wouldn't interrupt anyone. It didn't seem as far going by the road instead of cutting through the fields behind the church. Within twenty minutes she was turning in at the gate, and in another five, she was knocking on the back door. Mr Roberts opened the door, and looked at her in dismay.

'Why, Miss, you ought to have used the front door!'

She apologised, adding, 'I didn't want to be a bother, in the circumstances.' She explained why she was there, and the belt was quickly found. As she was preparing to take her leave, she heard a commotion of yapping and children shouting. Almost immediately, the two boys charged through the hall to the garden door, close on the heels of Gustave, with Madame Bovary panting past about ten seconds later, her stout form not able to keep up with the others. Dottie, desperately curious, nevertheless kept her questions to herself, feeling quite proud of how grown-up she was these days. She said good evening to Mr Roberts, and, squeezing past the two large trunks, locked, belted and stacked just inside the back door, she went on her way, her thoughts very busy.

As she came back into the village, two men, large and loud, almost cannoned into her. The large one paused to raise his battered hat in apology, but without missing a beat, resumed his conversation. Dottie overheard more than she bargained for.

'I walloped him one this time. 'Hardy, you keep away from my wife', I told him, and I whacked him right in the face. That'll teach him. He won't mess with me again. Nor ma missus.'

'No, he won't, Big Billy, that's for sure.'

'Asleep in his room he was, at The Thistle. Well, I hope he's learned his lesson. The look on his face! He went down like a nine-pin.' With his hands Big Billy mimed something crashing backwards, then gave a hearty laugh.

'You weren't the only one looking for him. There was that bookmaker the other day.'

'Oh aye, I know!' Another hearty laugh. 'I was there when he found him. Smacked him right on the nose, he did, just as he was coming into my bar. My bar, of all places. The laddie has a death wish!'

So, it was true! Dottie couldn't catch her breath. Her hands covered her mouth. Devastated, her one thought was to get to her room. She fought her way up the steps and inside the inn, reaching the hall, only to bump into the last person she wanted to see.

'Dottie!' said William, the bruises on his face illuminated by a chance ray of sunlight. 'I've been trying to find you. I need to tell you...'

'Oh you—you!' Words failed her, and so she lashed out with her hand, the palm of it stinging across his face with all the might she had. Tears blinded her and she turned and ran up the stairs in the direction of the bathroom.

His cheek was still stinging from her slap. It wasn't the first time she had slapped him. But the way she'd looked at him! His heart whispered that he had lost her forever, though his mind said fiercely that it wasn't so, that he would never, ever, let her go.

But was it even his decision to make? She'd slapped him, turned on her heel and stormed away, fury in every line of her tall, slender frame.

He went into the bar, abruptly halting in the doorway at the sight of the large figure propped against the counter. He was the last person William wanted to see right now, and he was, indirectly, the cause of all William's problems. William halted, and debated whether to throw caution to the wind and go in there and tell the man exactly what he thought of him. After all, he had nothing left to lose.

Nelson the landlord went by, lifting the flap to the bar and taking up his position, a glass and a cloth in his hands immediately. He gave a mocking wince as he looked at William's face. 'Ooh that looks nasty, Mr Hardy, sir. Your young lady certainly didn't hold back, did she?'

William glared at him and said nothing. He had enough to worry about as it was.

As if by some sixth sense aware of William's

presence, the man to his left man turned and looked right at him. After a second he laughed, loudly and unrestrained, and pointed at his own black eye and swollen lip.

'Now we're an even better match! Looks like we need to cheer each other up. What did the bard say, the course of true love never did run smooth? Let me get you a drink, man. Ye look like ye need it.'

Yet still he hesitated. Then all at once something inside him metaphorically threw up its hands in recognition of a pointless situation, and he gave in, and although still wary, he approached. A glass was pushed in front of him, a hand clapped his shoulder by way of sympathy.

He stood side by side with the brother he'd never known he had until the day before. In the mirror behind the bar he couldn't help but see they were a match in height and breadth of shoulder, in their hair colour and eyes. They could have been twins, both the image of their father. Only their clothes set them apart.

Will lifted his glance, gave William a broad grin, wincing at the pain and raised his free hand to soothe his eye. 'A toast. To the lovely ladies. The fair sex: gentle, kind, and loving. And who pack an almighty punch.'

William raised his glass. With a wry look, he echoed, 'To the ladies,' and drank his dram down in one gulp. It hit the spot and made him choke. He looked at Will. It was an odd sensation, thinking, 'This is my brother.'

Will looked back, his expression growing serious. 'All joking aside, man, I'm sorry I made trouble for you with your wife.'

'She's not my wife,' William said, adding with bitterness, 'And I don't suppose now she ever will be.'

'Och, hush man, faint heart never won a fair lady, and all that.'

'Do you do anything useful or do you only give quotations from literature?' William growled.

Will shot him a look, but wasn't offended. 'Aye, I can do this too.' And he signalled to Mr Nelson for another round, adding, 'O' course, if I'd had the same fancy education as my little brother, I'd probably do something a bit more useful with ma life.'

William was suddenly furious, and rounded on Will violently, his fists already balling up.

Will put a calming hand on William's chest, and in a soft voice said, 'I'm sorry, I'm sorry, I didnae mean that. I shouldnae have said it.'

Fresh drinks were placed in front of them, and William, shoving Will's hand aside, once again drank his down in one draught. He immediately signalled the barman.

Will said, 'Aye, a good plan. I can see you're the brains o' the family.' He added, 'It was me took you back to your room from the other bar, when Jimmy the Bookmaker decked you in mistake for me. I thought I owed you that much. Not as much as I owe Jimmy, o' course.'

William swore at him and sank the third whisky, and called for another. His cheek still stung from the pressure of Dottie's hand, and he decided he was going to drink until the pain went away, then he was going to tell her just what he thought about what she'd done.

He explained this to Will, who responded with another hearty shoulder slap and said, 'Aye, aye, another good plan. We need to tell those women what they've done to us. They're not the only ones to suffer, ya know. They seem to think we men have no feelings at all. How does she think I feel, huh, tell me that? I go to prison for a piddling twelve months and come back to find ma woman, the love o' ma life, married tae another man! Ma heart's in pieces, but does she care? Not a jot, let me tell ye, not a damned jot. Then she's the one that's upset?'

He raised his voice, 'Hey, barman, another round of drinks for me an' my brother!'

Peter Nelson stood in front of the pair of them, his arms folded across his chest. 'No more until I see some money on this counter.'

Will and William looked at the barman then at each other, and laughed hard, leaning on one another for support. The barman sighed. It was going to be a long evening.

Back in her room, Dottie was still weeping softly when she heard the tap on her door.

It couldn't be William, he'd never tap so softly, and in any case, given the mood he was in when she'd last seen him, he'd probably feel more inclined to kick the door off its hinges. She scrubbed at her cheeks with her handkerchief and went to see who was there.

She saw a small, slender woman with wavy red hair scooped back from her face in a loose bun, pretty wisps escaping and hanging about her neck.

Before Dottie had the chance to speak, the woman yelled in a loud, forceful way that belied her petite stature, 'You can keep away from ma man! You've no been in the neighbourhood two minutes and you're already after him! What sort of woman are you? Taking other peoples' men...'

But at this point, the forceful manner that had supported her thus far, fell away and the woman's voice caught in her throat, her eyes filled with tears.

Dottie looked up and down the corridor, then

took the woman's arm and pulled her into the room, shutting the door. 'I don't know what you're talking about,' she hissed bluntly. 'I've enough problems with my own man to keep me busy, I've no time for yours as well.'

'Is it William Hardy?' The woman was looking at her oddly. Dottie knew she too looked as though she'd been crying. The other woman hadn't missed her reddened eyes, or the damp handkerchief in her hand. But at the mention of his name, Dottie felt cold inside.

'What if it is?' she demanded. 'And anyway, what business is it of yours? You're married to that enormous fellow from the bar on the other side of the road.'

The woman nodded. Her eyes were full of sorrow. Her fingers twisted and untwisted in front of her, working at the edge of her apron. 'Aye. I am. I'm married to Big Billy McHugh, for better or for worse, according to the wedding vows, and it's been worse for this whole six months. I was a fool to marry him, but I just wanted to feel—safe. Mad, really, for I've never been less safe than I am with him. Very fast with his fists and his belt is Billy. But Will, he's never one to be where he's supposed to be or do what he's supposed to do. You can't rely on the man. Yet all the same, I love him.'

They sat on opposite sides of the bed, staring at each other. Dottie's head held a hundred questions. She asked the first, most pressing one. 'But how do you even know him?'

'I met him when he came into the bar. I was just a barmaid then. But after what's happened, he's no longer welcome these days. My husband hates him with a passion. I'm afraid if he ever catches him, he'll kill Will. But I cannae keep away from him, he's the only good thing in my life. When he's not passed out from the drink or locked up in prison, that is.'

'But I don't see how that can be...' Dottie was confused. Were they definitely talking about the same man? 'He only came here from London a few days ago. He's been in London for years.'

It was the other woman's turn to stare. She shook her head, trying to make sense of Dottie's words. 'No. The only man who's come here in the last few days from London that I've heard of, is that policeman fellow, the one who got punched in the face by mistake.'

Relief flooded Dottie. Suddenly everything began to make sense in her brain. She wasn't one hundred per cent certain, but she was almost there, and her confidence began to return. She just needed to make absolutely sure.

'This London policeman,' said Dottie. 'Have you actually seen him?'

The other woman shook her head. 'No, I just heard that he'd arrived. I havenae seen him with my own eyes. But Big Billy said this fellow got punched in the face as he came in the bar.'

'His name,' Dottie said, 'is William Hardy. He's my William Hardy. At least, he was mine until I slapped him half an hour ago. I doubt he'll ever speak to me again after that.'

'Will...?' The other woman was still staring at Dottie, but her eyes were wide as her mind raced over what Dottie had said. 'The London policeman is called William Hardy?'

'Yes, I just said so.'

'And he's your man?'

'Well... in a manner of speaking... yes, I suppose he is.'

'And you're not trying to take my Will Hardy?'

Dottie was confused again. 'But your man, I mean, your husband is Billy McHugh. Isn't he?'

'No. I'm married to Billy McHugh, but I love Will Hardy. Will is my man.'

Dottie felt this wasn't the moment to try and explain it was supposed to be one and the same man you both married and loved. 'Well I love my William Hardy from London, not your Will Hardy, and...' Dottie stopped short and thought about what she'd just said. 'Oh dear, I think I've just...' She searched for her handkerchief and scrubbed at her face again. After a moment she said, 'The thing is, I've just given him such a slap, all because I'd overheard someone outside talking and laughing about how he'd punched William Hardy in the face because he had been running after his wife. And I thought... I thought...'

She ground to a halt. She looked down at her hands, concentrating on the lamentable state of her nails, biting her lip to keep it from trembling. If she ignored her feelings, she might avoid another outbreak of tears. She had made a huge mistake, that was all too clear now. But it hadn't been him, it had been someone else. It helped a little bit to know that. Not her William, running around after married women. Unable to keep his trews on.

Though she had still slapped him.

'I'm Anna. Anna McHugh. And my man is definitely Will Hardy. He hates to be called William. And he has definitely lived here for years, though he's talked a lot of hot air about getting away from here. But between you and me, he will have to leave soon, or he'll likely spend the rest of his days behind bars, or even hang, because they are set to have him for that killing up at the big house.' She looked at Dottie. 'Two men with the same name. That's a bit unusual.'

Dottie sighed. 'Yes, it is. But there's a simple explanation. You see, I think they're brothers. Half-brothers, actually. The London one has been sent here to find the Scottish one, though I don't think he realised that until today. I know it sounds a bit of a muddle. I knew your Will's mother, and so I agreed when I was asked to come here to find him, to let him know that she has passed away, and ask him to contact her solicitor. You see, my William and I, we each only had half of the clue. Presumably to make us work together, and perhaps even to help us to fall for one another. But it's been a bit of a disaster so far.'

Anna sighed too. 'My Will's a hard one to track down. He's always trying to stay one step ahead of the law, that's what it is. And one step ahead of my husband. Will's such a one for getting into trouble. Always in some scrape or another. If he's not careful...' Anna looked at Dottie. It was a deep appraising look, as if trying to gauge something about her.

Dottie countered the look with one of her own.

Anna nodded. She'd made up her mind. 'Will you help me? I'm afraid he's got himself into some real trouble this time. I don't want him to go to prison. If they hanged him for this, it'd be the death of me too. Oh I know he's done a bit of poaching and he's a bit light-fingered, but he's never been really bad. He would never harm anyone or commit an actual crime.'

Again, Dottie saw no point in explaining that poaching and theft were actual crimes. Clearly where this Will fellow was concerned, Anna was determined to keep her rosy outlook. It was clear too that Anna was genuinely worried.

'You can tell me anything,' Dottie said. 'And if I can help at all, I promise I'll try.'

*

Day Six: Sunday

William Hardy didn't remember getting to bed the night before, and judging by the pounding of his head, there was a fundamental reason for that.

His body ached, his eyes felt glued shut, his mouth bore a resemblance to the gritty floor of the proverbial parrot's cage.

Slowly, and with great care, he hauled himself into a sitting position. It felt like a huge achievement, and his head swam with the effort. The pounding increased. He needed a large glass of cold water.

Wracking his brains, he remembered the bathroom was just along the corridor to the left. After a few moments of trying to ready himself for the journey, he swung his feet round to the floor, preparing for the attempt to stand. His foot struck something soft. Looking down, he saw his half-brother lying on his back on the floor, his coat folded under his head for a pillow.

This new discovery explained something else, too.

The terrible snorting noise that had been deafening him and that he had, up to now, taken for part and parcel of his hangover... It was, after all, only the sound of his drunk brother sleeping off the night before.

William shuffled along the bed, planted both feet firmly on the threadbare carpet, and clinging to the bedpost, bit by bit hoisted himself onto his feet. In doing so he almost dislodged the brown envelope from its place resting on the top of his open suitcase on the tallboy. He just managed to catch it and put it back on the pile of clothes Dottie had so neatly folded.

He teetered there. For a brief time he wasn't convinced he could walk at all, but then his brother belched loudly, and necessity propelled William out of the bedroom, along the corridor and into the bathroom at a far more rapid speed than was usual.

Ten minutes later, having poured a jug of icy water over his head and drunk a similar quantity from a tooth-glass, he emerged into the hallway, still shaky but feeling slightly more human.

The first person he met was Dottie Manderson. The curling of her lip as she took in his dishevelled appearance told him all he needed to know. His wits were too dull to form any kind of explanation or apology. He mumbled something indistinct and shambled away to his room.

Which was now empty.

On the bed was a torn scrap of paper. In a surprisingly neat hand Will had written, 'Meet me in Mason's Field, 11pm, tonight, and I'll sign your paper for you. I've some things I need to do before then.'

He had a vague memory of pouring out his story to his brother at some point. They'd come up to his room with a bottle, and he'd tried to get Will to sign the paper there and then. He remembered rummaging in the big envelope to find the smaller one, almost spilling the money everywhere, then remembering the paper was in his pocket after all, somewhat creased and the worse for wear.

But Will had said he wanted to sleep on it, though apparently he had since made up his mind. If it seemed an odd place to meet, William didn't care. Will Hardy would sign the paper, and William Hardy could go back to London and take that paper to Mr Bray and claim his remaining £250. That was all that mattered to him at this moment.

That, and getting a bit more sleep. He really wasn't feeling too well.

An hour later, and William Hardy was called to the telephone. The hour's sleep had done little to redress the excesses of the night before, and he was thankful Maple couldn't see him. They exchanged pleasantries and then:

'I've found out your information,' Maple said. 'It weren't easy, let me tell you. Seems Mr Denholme was a friend of one of the top brass, and he spoke to this friend about what was going on up in Scotland, and asked for help. Then, well, long story short, when the assistant commander found out you was on your way up here, he decided you could do him a favour. Two birds, one stone, like. The memo's on your desk. Clearly they forgot that if you was going away, you wouldn't be in the office collecting your messages.'

Hardy swore under his breath. 'Thanks, Frank. At least that takes care of something that was worrying me. That's all I needed to know.'

'It seems your fellow made a few dodgy investments and lost a lot of money recently. He's been fobbing off a lot of people with promises of a payment soon. So that might be a help to you. And the assistant commander said he wants to have a word with you next week, he wants to know what happened up there.'

'Don't we all,' Hardy said with feeling.

'Another thing, don't know if it'll be of use to you. But because the murder was reported in the newspapers here, a chap came into the public desk and left a message for 'Whoever is investigating the death of Howard Denholme', so it got passed along to me.'

Hardy was all ears. 'Go on.'

'Said he'd been hired by Mr Denholme to follow his wife.'

Hardy let out a low whistle. 'I was told the lady never ventures out, due to onerous domestic duties and a violent husband.'

'Hmm, apart from to consult with her doctor on some minor health issues. Though she's not been going to her doctor. This man was a private enquiry agent, and he's been following her for three months. It seems once a month she's been meeting up with a certain procurator fiscal for a day of fun and frolics at a small, and very discreet, very expensive hotel in Edinburgh. He's promised to develop another set of the photographs he sent to Mr Denholme two weeks ago, and bring them in to us.'

It all fell neatly into place in Hardy's mind. There was nothing further, so Hardy, with a clear sense of triumph, thanked him and said goodbye.

Dottie reflected that there was a good turn-out at the church for the morning's service. Thank goodness she had packed a sensible skirt and coat, though. The sun might be shining outside, but here inside the shadowy stone church, it was freezing.

She wasn't surprised that Mrs Denholme and the boys were not in church. She exchanged smiles and nods with the butler and his wife, and the young maid. At the end of the service, Dottie spied Anna McHugh seated in a pew at the back of the church. She waited whilst Anna spoke to a couple of people before coming over to Dottie.

'Let's go somewhere and have a chat,' Dottie said. 'There are a few things I want to tell you.'

They sat on a bench in a corner of the churchyard. Anna, agitated, didn't give Dottie a chance to say anything, but rushed into speech.

'He has no alibi!' She stifled a sob. A hundred yards away, a small group of people were waiting respectfully by a grave as an elderly woman placed flowers upon it. Anna went on, 'Any other time, he'd have been wi' me, but with Big Billy so angry... Well, he knows now what's been going on, thanks to Will telling the police about me last time they pulled him in about some poaching. Now Big Billy watches me like a hawk. So he knows I was in the kitchen the whole evening, making food for the customers, and I can't make something up.'

'Will has no alibi?' Dottie repeated. She was deep in thought. Anna clutched at her arm.

'He would never kill anyone. He wouldn't do such a thing. I mean, I know he's bad, but...'

'I know.' Dottie patted her hand. 'We'll think of something. Do you know where to find him? I need to talk to him. It's urgent.'

Anna shot her an interested look, but simply nodded and said, 'Aye, I know where he is. Will we go there now?'

'Yes, let's,' Dottie said, making up her mind. It was time she introduced herself to Mrs Carmichael's son.

But he wasn't there. He was not in any of his usual haunts, and Dottie, in addition to Anna, began to fear the police had already apprehended him. She went back to the inn to look for William.

She found him on his way down from his room, looking pale but considerably better than when she'd seen him earlier. He suggested they drive to Edinburgh and eat lunch in comfort. They said little on the journey. Dottie was planning what she wanted to tell him and pondering the best way to tell it. If she had wondered at his silence, she might have been surprised to learn that he was doing the same thing. Each of them was glad to be spending some time in what felt like neutral territory.

The hotel's restaurant was busy, but there was room for two more diners at a small out-of-the-way table. With the noise of conversation and the staff coming and going, they were effectively as alone as if they had been on a deserted island. They ordered their food, and observed each other warily.

'I'm booked on tomorrow morning's ten o'clock train back to London,' William said as an opener. Whatever she had expected, it hadn't been that.

'Oh.' She thought a moment and said, 'Then I could probably go back tomorrow as well. There's not really much more I can do here. I'll ring up and reserve a seat when we get back to The Thistle.'

'I could do that,' he said.

'There's no need, William, I can do it. Thank you anyway. Let me know your seat number.'

The waiter appeared to pour them some wine. There was a rigmarole of William tasting and then approving the vintage. What would happen, Dottie thought, if everyone just started sending their wine back? Almost no one ever did. It was taken for granted that the wine was everything it should be. The waiter appeared oblivious to the tension at their table.

'I want you to meet someone,' she said as soon as the waiter had left them. William immediately shook his head. She laughed gently, and put a hand on his arm. 'Silly! You don't even know who I want you to meet.'

'I expect it's my half-brother,' he said. 'I've already met him, and I've no intention of meeting him again.'

Dottie stared at him. 'You can't possibly mean that. William, he's your brother, and he needs your help.'

He gave her a cool look that she didn't much like, and she suddenly realised their pleasant meal was over.

'No,' he said. 'He's a stranger. I barely know the man. I'm only here because I need to get his signature on the paper Mr Bray gave me. And he's going to sign that paper for me tonight. I'm to meet him at eleven o'clock tonight. Then I'm getting on that train tomorrow morning and I'm going home. I don't intend to forge some kind of bond with the man. He's nothing to me. And I hope he stays that way.'

Dottie was seriously tempted to throw her wine in his face, but instead, and feeling quite calm and grown-up about it, she got up and said, 'Excuse me, William, I think I shall leave now.' And before he could say another word, she walked out of the hotel and hailed a taxi.

Everyone turned to look at William Hardy, the man with the badly bruised face and even more badly bruised ego. He put his head in his hands.

Mason's Field was less of a field in the usual sense, and more of an extensive boggy trap for the ankles of the unwary, William Hardy quickly discovered. The night was a cloudy one, now drizzling, now gusting a chilly wind. It was impossible to believe summer was a mere month away. He trudged across the field, cursing himself for not having the foresight to bring gumboots, and keeping a look-out for his half-brother, and at the same time, for potholes.

It occurred to him now—far too late—that the middle of a field at eleven o'clock at night was not after all the best place to expect anyone to sign a document. He halted beneath a tree and scanned the gloom for any trace of movement. Shadows pitched and tossed as the branches of the trees swayed and undulated in the wind, and the moon disappeared then re-emerged from behind dark clouds framed against an even darker sky. A fresh downpour distracted him. He was busy turning up his coat collar to protect himself from the weather, taking a step back under the shelter of the tree, when a sudden surging movement in the darkness nearby made him start. At the same time, a low voice said,

'Well, don't just stand there, take this and run!'

A heavy rough sack was bundled into his arms, and too surprised to refuse it or drop it, he clutched it and ran after Will's ghostly form, pelting through the shadows. He believed his half-brother to be about twenty or thirty feet ahead, though the moon chose that moment to disappear again, and it was difficult to be precise. An angry shout from behind them came to William's ears, borne on the wind, and he naturally put on a spurt.

It felt like a game. From in front, Will urged him on, disappearing through the gate and out into the lane. William, sensing the pursuers closing in, tore through the gate, round the curve of the hedge, and threw himself abruptly to the left, into the ditch, lying still and low, hushing his panting breath as the men rushed by without seeing him, their feet on a level with his head.

A quick, jubilant, youthful sense of victory came over him and he wanted to laugh. He wanted to run and run and run. How many years had it been since he had simply just run for the sheer joy of doing so? He felt all the energy of childhood rushing through him like the blood in his veins, and excitement seemed to flood his whole being.

He hid the sack—with the whatever-it-was—under a sprawling bush on the lip of the ditch and hauled himself up and out onto the lane. He brushed himself down and set off down the road, at a lazy stroll. He whistled loudly as he went.

Within a minute or two, the men came running back. One shone a torch in his face while the other, brandishing a shotgun, demanded to know his business.

He introduced himself, quite truthfully, as Inspector William Hardy of the London Metropolitan Police. He produced his warrant card and before they could comment on his name, told them plainly what he thought about having a shotgun aimed at him.

'Sorry, sir, we didn't know. But we was on the track of a poacher. He's been running rings round us. We chased him through here not five minutes ago. And this is not even loaded,' the fellow with the shotgun said, digging in his pockets for the loose shells. He broke the shotgun to show William the empty chambers.

'Well, it's hardly likely to be me, is it?' William said without so much as a blush. 'After all I only arrived from London three days ago.'

They admitted the apparent truth of this, and apologised once more. One of the men shone his torch in Hardy's face again and, nodding at the bruises, said, 'Did your wife do that to you, laddie?'

Hardy smiled. 'Yes, she did,' he said.

They laughed merrily then went on their way, bidding him a good night. He felt guilty, although his involvement had been unwitting, but as he went back to the village, he couldn't help laughing over the childish caper. His mood was light and joyful.

By the time he reached the village street, the rain had stopped, the wind had blown away the clouds, and the moon shone brightly down, bathing all the country with silver threads. It seemed magical, and he was so glad to be outside, so glad to be alive. Here you could breathe, and there was not another soul on the road. He gulped in the night air, enjoying the cold feeling of it going down into his body. He began to whistle again, but softly now.

As he drew near the inn, he noted the deeper shadow beyond the sign, the trunk of the copper beech there appearing twice as wide as usual. As he approached, part of it seemed to detach itself and come towards him.

'You're a cool one, you are, I have tae say,' Will said. 'Don't tell me you've give 'em their geese back.'

William laughed. If Will was surprised to hear it, he said nothing.

William shook his head. 'So that's what was in the sack. I can't believe you left me to get caught with them. But no, luckily for you, and for myself, I had my wits about me. I left them for you. You'll find them easily enough if a fox doesn't get them first.' And he told Will where to find them, adding, 'Now, if you'll just sign my paper, our business will be concluded.'

It was Will's turn to laugh. 'I'm signing nothing,' he said, and turned and walked away.

William let him go. He was neither surprised nor angry. He shrugged his shoulders and went into The Thistle. He headed straight upstairs.

Outside, Will stood smoking a cigarette further along the road under the canopy of the tree as was his custom, and watched him go. He felt puzzled by his brother's easy acceptance of his refusal. When he went back to the lane, to the ditch, he found the sack there with the two geese carcasses, just as William had said. He was not sure what to make of it.

He was meeting Anna. She'd promised to slip out to spend some time with him. They made themselves comfortable inside a barn. There was a bed of old straw, dusty but dry. She was there when he arrived, and in his arms as soon as he called her name.

'I need to talk to ye,' she said, pushing him away when he tried to close in for another kiss. 'Sit yeself down. It'll take a while.'

'I need to tell you something too. I've got a brother.' He heard the pride in his voice as he spoke. He heard the soft sound of her laugh.

'I know! I met the girl who loves him. She told me everything. Why he's here, why she's here. You need to talk to him. You've got to sign a paper he has. You've got an inheritance to claim!'

He was silent for a minute or two. She nudged him, and he put his arms around her, pulling her back with him into the straw.

'There's just two problems wi' that,' he admitted. 'One, the procurator is trying to bring me in for the murder of Howard Denholme.'

'I know you'd never do such a thing!' she exclaimed.

'I've never killed a man, and would never do it unless it was to protect you or our bairns.'

'Our bairns?' she repeated softly. He kissed her.

'Of course, our bairns.' There was a passionate interlude. Finally, she pushed him away and said, 'And what was the second problem?'

'I took ma brother's money. I cannae see him again now.'

'What!' She sat bolt upright. 'How could you do such a ridiculous thing?' She slapped him hard across the shoulder, the closest part of him within range. 'You fool! Worse than a fool! Your own brother!'

He buried his face against her. 'I know, I know, I just saw it there, an envelope with a big pile of banknotes inside, and...' He groaned. 'I couldnae help it. I was thinking you and me could get away. But now—I wish I hadn't done it. What can I do?'

'Ye've got to give it back. That's obvious, surely?'

'I can't face him...'

'Give the money to me, I'll give it to her and she can give it to him,' she said patiently. 'Easy.'

'But...'

'Then, you'll sign his paper, claim your inheritance and you can lie low until they catch the real murderer.'

'Aye, well, they'll only do that if they look for the beggar in the first place.'

Constable Forbes got himself comfortable, his back firmly wedged against a tree-trunk, and got out his thermos of tea laced with a little something extra. He poured himself a nice hot drink. Summer wasn't far off, but at any time of year it was common for a cool breeze to come inland at night off the sea. The tea was too hot to drink immediately, but he knew Hardy and Anna McHugh were going to be busy a while yet, so he had plenty of time. He unwrapped his sandwiches and took a huge chunk out of the first one, the flavour of beef and sliced raw onion hitting his appreciative tastebuds.

He didn't mind being on duty at night if it meant sitting quietly somewhere and having a nice picnic. He had been keen to help Inspector Hardy by keeping an eye on young Will. If anyone came to arrest the young ne'er-do-weel, he was to let the Englishman know right away. Since the London inspector had arrived a few days earlier, Forbes' experience of policing had changed drastically. Now it was full of big-city-type crime and here he was 'tailing' suspects to report on their whereabouts. He might even consider a transfer to a busier police station, do some real policing. Life suddenly seemed full of exciting possibilities. And tea and sandwiches.

Inside the inn, on the landing outside the guest rooms, William came face to face with Dottie. She still looked pale and upset, he thought. But all she said was, 'Been out again?' in a rather offhand voice.

'Yes. Just fancied a walk.'

'Country air is reputed to help one to sleep.' She sounded at her most haughty, he thought, but was as lovely as ever.

Clearly, she was still furious with him. But he was too tired to fight with her. Instead he gave her a gentle smile and said, simply, 'Yes indeed, very bracing. Such a pleasant change from London.' If she could be like that, he could too.

'Why've you got mud on your coat?'

He turned to look down at his sleeve and side. 'Oh. Well, I don't know the roads too well, so unfortunately I fell into a ditch.'

'Good!' She turned and walked away. She felt very annoyed to hear him laughing softly behind her. She slammed her door rather loudly, and locked it for good measure. Then pulled the chair across in front of it, even though she knew she was being ridiculous. The actions did little to calm her temper.

He returned to his room to collect his things for a much-needed bath. At first, he noticed nothing awry, but then he pushed aside the brown envelope from Mr Bray to reach his washing things, and realised the envelope was empty. The money—his £250—had gone. And he knew exactly who had taken it.

An hour later, Dottie answered a knock at her door, half-expecting it to be William. She'd hoped he would come to make it up with her. But it wasn't him. Anna stood there, looking anxious, and beside her stood the man Dottie had come to Scotland to meet.

It was an odd sensation, looking into the eyes of a man whose face she knew so well, yet seeing him regard her as a stranger. She stepped back from the door and invited them into the room.

She put out a hand to shake his, but instead he captured it between both of his and carried it to his lips, his eyes laughing at her over their clasped hands.

'Ma pleasure, I'm sure,' he said, and even in those few words, the Scottish burr was clear.

Dottie removed her hand, raised an eyebrow at the glowering Anna, and said with a little too much candour, 'You've got your work cut out with this one.'

'Aye, and don't I know it!' Anna slapped him on the arm. He laughed, not in the least concerned. Dottie shook her head. He looked so like William, she could hardly believe it wasn't him. His clothes were different, his hair needed cutting, but it was the same fair shade. His eyes, his height, his build. Even the timbre of his voice. It was William. Just not her William.

Setting her thoughts aside, in as few words as possible, Dottie told him the news she had come all that way to deliver.

He nodded, saying nothing, just continued to lean against the window frame, staring out at the street. He'd already heard it all before. Anna said, excitement in her voice, 'So what is this inheritance?'

'I'm afraid I don't know,' Dottie said. She wrote on a piece of paper and gave it to Anna. 'This is Mr Bray's address in London. You must contact him, and he will tell you the rest.'

'That policeman has the paper for me to sign. So I can get ma inheritance. I said I would do it, but I changed ma mind,' Will said over his shoulder.

Dottie was hurt that he referred to her own William in such a way. She glanced at Anna for an explanation.

'He's got something he needs to tell you. He's done something stupid. As usual.'

Will didn't move or speak. Anna raised her voice slightly, 'Haven't you?' She turned back to Dottie. 'That's why he's sulking like a wee girl.'

Dottie looked at them both and waited. After a few seconds, with a sigh, Will turned, and Dottie saw he had tears in his eyes. He pulled out a none-too-clean handkerchief from his pocket and handed it to her.

'He'll never speak to me again. I took this from his room this morning. Ma own brother. I took ma own brother's money.'

Dottie untied the handkerchief and saw a messy pile of banknotes.

'It's easy,' Dottie said. 'Sign this piece of paper

and while you're doing that, I'll put the money in his room with a note. He's going back to London tomorrow morning, as am I. This piece of paper is all he came here for—the solicitor sent him up here so that the two of you could meet and find out about each other. I suppose Mr Bray thought the two of you would get on, be proper brothers. But it's looking as though that was just wishful thinking. You can't make people like one another. But he came all this way, and he got punched in the face twice instead of you, and he's been trying to find out who killed that Mr Denholme, so the least you can do, for yourself and for him, is to sign this dratted paper.'

With a grudging respect, Will quickly wrote down just what she told him to write, and signed the page with a flourish. Dottie added the date and her own signature as witness. She put the paper safely away in her handbag.

'And now your note for William,' she said, and her tone brooked no refusal. 'You owe him this much.'

He wrote a note, stating the bad facts: He had taken the money. He shouldn't have. He was sorry. He was giving it back.

'Right,' she said. She unlocked the connecting door, and opened the door on William's side, still unlocked, and she went in, placed the package of money and the note of apology on his bed, then came back out.

She looked at Anna and Will. 'See? Easy.'

*

Day Seven: Monday

The coast hadn't been clear after all.

Will Hardy had got out of the barn, and tiptoed right past the sleeping Constable Forbes. Will had wondered about giving him a gentle kick to wake him up. The man had been there all night, surely he'd have a stiff neck by now.

It had seemed rather a good joke to walk right past the constable, but almost immediately Will stopped in his tracks at the sound of an approaching vehicle. It was a police car. This had to be the Edinburgh police come for him. He stepped behind the tree that supported Forbes' back, hoping that the driver and passengers hadn't seen him. The constable stretched and yawned and got to his feet. He exchanged a few words with the men in the car, and was chastised for his trouble. He went to pick up his bicycle to go back to the police house.

As soon as the car was out of sight, and not sure where else to go, Will made his way to Mason's Field, unaware that Forbes had seen him go.

An hour later, and Will was watching from his position crouched in the heather. He watched as William come into view, and stood looking about him, his hand going up to protect his eyes from the thin but persistent sunlight.

Will was fairly sure he was safe where he was. At least his brother was alone. Which meant he hadn't given him up to the men from Edinburgh—yet. He was confident William would not try to find him. Surrounded by the vast expanse of moorland, on every side he would be confronted by the same vista stretching towards the horizon. Where could anyone make a start? There was too much landscape, too many nooks and crannies, too much heather and rock for one man to search. So long as Will remained where he was, he was safe, even though he was close enough to have hit William with a pebble. If he waited patiently, William would just give up and leave.

What surprised him was that William began to speak. He didn't shout. No, he pitched his voice only slightly above his normal volume. That surprised Will. Clearly then, his half-brother knew he was close at hand. Will smiled to himself. His brother was quick, that was for sure. He had to admire that. He listened, less and less certain now that he was as securely hidden as he had thought.

'I know you're there. I know you can hear me. I just wanted to say that I'm going back to London. I'm getting the bus from the crossroads. I'm leaving the rented car. You'll need it to get away from the Edinburgh police. I'm not going to come after you. As far as anyone knows, you overpowered me and took the car. I will keep working to prove your innocence, meanwhile you must get away somewhere overseas, both you and Anna. Make a new start, with my blessing. I know we've had our differences, but after all we are brothers. I-I suppose I'm glad I had the chance to get to know you just a little. If you ever need anything, you can find me through Mr Bray. Just—please—let me know when you arrive safely at, well, wherever it is you end up—and—well—Godspeed.'

There was a long moment's silence before William turned and walked away, back down the lane, pausing briefly to collect his suitcase from the car. Then he set off resolutely down the hill towards the crossroads and the bus-stop to town.

Will got to his feet and watched him go. If William had turned at that point, he would have seen him standing there, he couldn't have missed seeing him. But he didn't turn back, and Will watched him go until the curve of the landscape swallowed him from view. There was a lump in Will's throat, and he had a mad urge to run after him, but he forced it down and made his way to the car, clambering over rocks and heathery tussocks, slipping and sliding, until he reached the vehicle.

He glanced about him, checking neither William nor anyone else was nearby. He peered inside the car. On the back seat was the large brown envelope. That surprised him too, as it seemed to him William was not the forgetful type. Opening the back door and leaning inside, careful not to bump his head, he picked up the envelope and looked inside. He gave a low whistle, a chuckle, hurriedly closed the flap again and placed the envelope in the footwell, under his jacket.

It was too good an opportunity to miss. He yanked open the door and jumping into the driver's seat, he started the car. He rolled it slowly down the little hill, over the uneven ground, gathering a little speed as it came out onto the road proper.

Sure enough, there was William still hiking to the bus-stop. What if he were to stop and offer him a lift? For a second he almost stopped, amused by the idea. But he was undecided, and the car kept going, and before he'd properly made up his mind, he was already running past William. He saw William half-turn as he drove by, but Will turned his head away, not wanting to meet William's eyes. At the crossroads Will turned the car north, towards the village and the coast beyond.

There was a full tank of petrol, he noticed. Again he smiled. Just because William was a copper didn't mean he wasn't a good man. William had been right, it had been good to meet, to spend a brief bit of time together. It was good to know that he wasn't alone in the world. Perhaps someday, hopefully not too far off in the future, they'd have another chance to get to know one another.

He stopped the car. He got out and stared back along the road, waiting. After a few minutes, he saw William coming down towards the crossroads. He halted in his tracks on seeing the car with Will standing beside it, leaning negligently on the front wing. They stared at one another across a hundred yards of road.

In the distance, Will could hear the sound of an engine. William had planned his timing perfectly to fit with the one bus per day into Edinburgh. The bus appeared on the ridge behind Will, and William, turning away, hurried to meet it at the stopping point.

Will watched him get into the bus. After a few seconds the bus pulled away, and Will was never quite sure whether or not he imagined the face at the back window, and the hand that waved goodbye.

He pulled the car up outside The Dirk, taking care to leave the engine running in case a quick getaway was required. It usually was, in his experience. He sounded the horn. A couple of curtains twitched in cottage windows but other than that, nothing happened. Never a patient man, he honked again. Twice. More curtains twitched, and finally the pub door was thrown open. Big Billy McHugh filled the space with his huge shoulders and even huger belly.

'Get out of here!' he yelled. 'No one wants you here. Get away before I set the cops on ye. Or better yet, I'll teach you a lesson maself. Run off with your tail between your legs, like you did last time.'

Will said nothing, did nothing. Billy McHugh wasn't quite ready to step aside, however. Pulling off his apron and throwing it on the ground, he stepped out into the street, pushing up his sleeves as if preparing for a fight.

Will smiled and let down his window. He could never compete with Billy McHugh in a boxing competition, but that wasn't what this was about. It wasn't about having a fist-fight to see which of them could defeat the other. Billy seemed to be the only one who didn't know that.

Someone small with bright red hair pushed past the barman. Anna. Ignoring her husband, now yelling at her to get back inside the bar 'where she belonged', she strolled over to the car and leaning against the door, her arms folded, said very casually, 'So Will, what are you doing today?'

'Oh, I'm just going for a little ride, taking in some scenery, enjoying the country air, you know the kind of thing.' He winked at her.

'Aye, very nice too. You've got a good day for it,' she replied. She was smiling, but he could see the pain in her eyes. And the new bruise marring her cheek. 'When are ye coming back?' she asked softly.

'I'm not,' he said. He saw shock in her eyes; she winced at his words. He didn't want to add to her pain, he just wanted to get her away from here. Forever. Raising his voice so that Billy McHugh could hear, he repeated, 'I'm no coming back. I'm leaving right now, and I won't ever be back here again.'

'Good riddance,' snarled McHugh, and a good deal more besides. Up and down the village street, people were opening windows and doors to hear what was going on.

'Isn't that the London policeman's car, the one he rented in Edinburgh?' Anna asked, looking it over as if for clues. She'd make a good police officer herself, Will thought.

He nodded. 'Aye, it is. I'm to take it back for him.'

'Good riddance to him an' all!' yelled McHugh, 'Poking his posh nose in where it's not wanted. Stirring up trouble for decent people, the nosy b...'

'Hey!' yelled Will, suddenly angry. 'That's ma brother you're talking about, so watch it!'

Anna leaned down to speak to him softly through the window. 'You'd better go, he's in a filthy temper. He's just looking for any excuse for a fight.'

'Let's give him one then,' said Will. He smiled at her. 'Give me a kiss.' He caught her unawares, leaning forward to plant a kiss full on her lips.

Fear flashed in her eyes. Behind her, Billy McHugh let out a howl of fury, his face turning bright red, and the man-mountain began to lumber towards the car. Anna yelped and ran around to the other side of the car. Will leaned across to open the door for her and at the same time, he let off the brake.

'Will!' she protested as they rolled away. He pushed down on the accelerator, the car shot forward and within seconds, Big Billy McHugh was reduced to a sorry spectacle of impotent rage behind them.

'I'm going to France, Mrs McHugh, and I want you to go with me.' He slowed the car now they were beyond the fringe of the village.

She gave him a look half-laughing, half-pleading. 'That's madness! How can I? I can't go to France.' In a whisper she added, 'Oh please don't say such things... If only...' Her eyes were full of tears. 'We can't. Or at least... I can't... You can, you're free to suit yourself, but I...'

'Why can't you?' he asked, his voice soft and urgent. 'Why can't you?' He tried to take her hand but she pushed him away.

'I'm no free, you know that, I can't just...'

'You can. You can if you really want to. Come with me, Anna. You can do it if it's what you want.' She was torn, he could see it. He didn't want to push her, but neither did he want to lose her now that they finally had this chance to be together. She cast a look about her, still caught halfway between laughter and fear.

'What are we supposed to live on? Have you even got any money?'

'Look in the back. Under the jacket.'

She lifted the sleeve of the jacket, picked up the envelope with a puzzled glance in Will's direction, then looked inside and saw the banknotes in their neat stacks. There was a plain, leather-strapped wristwatch there too. She stared at Will in disbelief. 'But... I-I don't understand. Didn't Dottie give the money back to him last night? We saw her take it into the room. Did you steal it again?'

'No, my love, he gave it to me. A wee gift from my brother. To help us start our new life together. And with his blessing.'

She sank back in the seat, staring ahead at the road, thinking. Then she said, 'But I've got no passport. I've no luggage, no clothes, not even a handkerchief to my name!'

He captured her hand and kissed it. 'That's what the money's for,' he explained patiently.

'But...' she said.

He turned to face her. 'Anna, this is it. You've got to choose. Either you can go back to being Billy McHugh's punchbag, or you can come with me to France. It's up to you. Are you a woman or a mouse?'

She gave him a look from under her lashes, and in a voice barely above a whisper said, 'Do you love me?'

'Oh, Anna...'

'But do you, Will? Do you really?'

He leaned across and kissed her on the mouth, gently to begin with, but with mounting passion. 'I love you, Anna McHugh. Don't make me go on ma own, I can't leave you behind again. I need you wi' me. Now, for the love of God, woman, choose!'

'Hmm. It's just so difficult to make up my mind. I'm so tempted to stay here with lovely Billy and continue to be beaten on a regular basis,' she laughed. 'What part of France are we going to?'

He only just made it in time to catch the train. As he raced along the platform, the guard was blowing his whistle and warning those on the platform to 'stand clear'. But William took no notice. As the train lurched and began to slowly move out of the station, he put on a spurt and lunged for the door handle nearest him, leaping onto the step. He had to lean back to wrestle open the door. The train gathered speed and passed the end of the platform. From his doorway further along the train, the guard furiously shouted, but William was inside, and had—just—made it.

The guard met William in the corridor and had a few choice things to say to him. 'That was very foolish, sir, very foolish. I've a good mind to report you. You can get fined for that kind of thing. There's a reason why...'

William, not particularly caring, pulled out his warrant card and cut him off, saying those magic words, 'I'm sorry but this is urgent police business.'

Immediately the guard was a friend, an interested friend who hoped to have a thrilling story to pass on to his friends and family later that evening. 'If there's anything I can do to help, Inspector, you only have to ask. I'm sure if there's anything I can do...'

'Thank you,' William said, catching his breath at last and putting away the warrant card he had so fraudulently used. He wondered if law-breaking was a trait that ran in his family after all. Oh well, he thought, in for a penny, in for a pound. 'I'm trying to track down a very pretty young woman. She's tall, slim, very pretty, with dark wavy hair. She's a well-to-do lady, likely to be travelling first class.'

'Is that her usual modus operandi? Like one of those exotic spies, travelling everywhere in the grandest style?' the guard asked. William said nothing and the man cleared his throat and concentrated on the job in hand. 'Come this way, sir, I think I might know who you mean. Saw her get on just now.' The guard turned to lead William back along the corridor, saying over his shoulder, 'What's she done?'

William immediately responded with a solemn,

'I'm afraid I can't tell you that. It's official police business and very hush-hush.'

'Of course, of course,' said the guard, enthralled but trying to act like this kind of thing happened on his trains every day. 'This way, sir.'

As the train gathered speed, they made their way unsteadily along the corridor until they came to the last first class compartment. William bumped into the man's back as he stood and looked through the glass. Stepping back from view, and pulling William with him, the guard said, 'There she is, sir, sitting there as calm as you like. For all the world as if she'd done nothing wrong. It fair takes your breath away, don't it? The nerve of these people!'

'Indeed. Um, best if you go back to your position, leave this to me,' William said.

With great reluctance, the guard did as he was told, after reminding William to use the emergency brake cord if he found himself in difficulties.

As soon as the coast was clear, William slid open the door and stepped inside. Dottie looked up and her eyes widened, but then she schooled her features and gave him a neutral, disinterested glance then looked away. In the opposite corner, a stout matron eyed William suspiciously.

'It's a non-smoker,' she warned him sternly, in a school-ma'am voice.

'Yes, I realise that. That's just what I want.' He replied as politely as he could when really he wanted to tell her to go and boil her head.

'Just so long as you know,' she said, clearly determined to set him in his place.

He sat down next to Dottie, who turned away slightly. 'Dottie...' he pleaded.

'Go away, William, I'm not talking to you.' She pulled a magazine out of her bag and began to flick through the pages.

'Dottie, if you'll just let me explain.'

'She said she's not talking to you, young man, so hop it,' chimed in the matron.

He glared at her. If she thought she could wade into people's private conversations, she could think again.

'Excuse me,' he said, and moved to sit on the other side of Dottie, with his back to the other woman, effectively blocking Dottie from her view. He attempted to capture Dottie's hand, but she snatched it free.

'Go away, William,' she hissed at him.

'Look, I just want to talk to you. I need to apologise, and I can't do that if you don't look at me, or let me hold your hand.' He watched her face for a moment, trying to make up his mind if she was in the mood to listen to him or if it was all just pointless. 'Dottie...' he added, in a soft pleading voice.

'Very well,' Dottie said haughtily in what he thought of as her mother's tone, 'You have two minutes. That's it.'

He took a deep calming breath and said very rapidly, 'Right. In that case, I want you to know I'm very sorry for what I said about my brother, and for upsetting you, and for doing everything wrong. I know I'm a prize idiot.'

From behind him the matron snorted and murmured, 'You can say that again. You're a man, aren't you?'

He ignored her and continued, his two minutes draining away, 'I should have listened to you; I know it was just pride that stopped me. Dottie, please don't be like this with me, I'm so very, very sorry.' He couldn't think of anything else to say, so he stopped, and waited, holding his breath for the metaphorical axe to fall.

'What about your brother?' she asked, turning another page of her magazine and scrutinising it carefully. He wasn't sure if he liked her asking about Will, but he simply said,

'I let him go. I told him to get away abroad somewhere with Anna. I gave him back the money to help him get started.'

She looked at him properly now for the first time. 'Oh William!' There was no mistaking the adoration in her voice. She leaned forward and was about to plant a kiss right on his lips, when the matron cleared her throat loudly and said:

'A time and a place. Carrying on in public like that. It ought to be illegal. When I was a girl, you'd have got arrested for public indecency. If I see a policeman, I'll tell him to throw you both off the train!'

William sat back against the seat, his eyes shutting momentarily in frustration.

Dottie said, 'Did you really let him go?'

He nodded.

'Do you think he'll definitely go back for Anna? She loves him deeply. I can't bear the thought of her pining away for Will, stuck in that awful pub with that awful Billy.'

'I'm sure he will. He loves her so much.'

She turned to face him. 'Did you make it up with him? I know it's hard for you to accept that he is your half-brother, but...'

'We understood each other in the end,' he said. 'Actually, I think it will be rather good to know he's out there somewhere. I asked him to keep in touch.'

'I'm so glad. And do you think he will? Keep in touch?' She took his hand, ignoring the matron's warning cough.

'I hope so. Perhaps not immediately. First I've got to prove he isn't a killer. But one day, yes, I think he will get in touch and hopefully we could meet up. Once it's safe. I'd like to introduce him to Eleanor and Edward and the rest of my family. Then no doubt he'll disappear again like the proverbial Scotch Mist.'

'By the way,' she said, rummaging in her handbag. 'This is for you. I know he didn't sign your paper, but Anna and I made him sign this, it should be just as good.' She put a slip of paper in his hand. There in a neat script were the same words that Mr Bray had written out on William's paper, and underneath, Dottie had signed as a witness, and his brother's name was written with a flourish beside the previous day's date.

'Oh Dottie!' He looked down at the paper. 'You have no idea what this means to me.'

Conversation was stilted due to the presence of the disapproving woman in the corner. However, after an hour or so of the gentle rocking motion of the train, the lady at last fell asleep, leaving Dottie and William effectively alone.

As soon as he realised the woman was asleep, his arm stole around Dottie's shoulders and he drew her closer to him, feeling rather daring as he planted a kiss on her hair as she leaned her head against him.

She looked up at him with her huge eyes, her lovely eyes that so bewitched him, and he had a sudden impulse. He slid off the seat onto his knees. Taking her hand, he gave her what he hoped was an irresistibly adorable look, and said, 'Dottie, darling, I love you so much. Please, would you do me the honour of...'

The train lurched over some points, he fell

forward onto Dottie's lap, the matron woke with a start and seizing her umbrella, brought it down on William's head and shoulders repeatedly, shouting, 'Get away from her, you brute! Guard! Guard!'

William, surging to his feet, was able to wrest the weapon from the woman's hands, and stammering a half-apology, half-explanation, he turned back to Dottie who was giggling uncontrollably. 'Dottie! Say something!' he pleaded as the matron started to scream even more loudly for the guard. If there was anything this 'romantic' moment didn't need, it was more people. He hauled Dottie to her feet and bundled her out into the corridor, slamming the door shut with rather more force than necessary and sending a warning look at the older woman. He turned back to Dottie, but his heart was sinking, the moment was gone. How could he recapture it?

She came into his arms and kissed his cheek, her gloved hands light on his shoulders. The train settled once more onto a smooth stretch of track, and William's heart sang. He put his arms around her and held her tight. Her cheek rested against his neck, her hair tickled his chin and above the sound of the engine, and more shouts from the older woman, he heard her softly say, 'Yes, William, I will marry you.'

He could hardly believe it. Taking half a step back, he looked into her eyes for confirmation. Her eyes were brimming with happy tears and lovelier than ever. He knew they would always bewitch and ensnare him.

'You will?'

She nodded. And laughed. 'I will!' A cloud seemed to pass over her face. 'You haven't changed your mind?'

'Never!' And he hugged her fiercely, not even noticing the woman dash past them to fetch the guard.

They remained at the corridor window, clutching the rail and talking, mainly nonsense, punctuated by the occasional chaste kiss. William longed to throw convention to the wind and really kiss her—but he just couldn't do that here where absolutely anyone might walk by and see them.

'There they are!'

William rolled his eyes. The matron was back with reinforcements in the shape of the guard and a couple of sturdy-looking ladies in large hats. Seeing William thus with his arms around Dottie, and in the process of placing another kiss on her cheek, the guard shouted.

'Oi! Stop that!'

Dottie laughed loudly, her hand going to her mouth. The guard fumbled for his whistle. The matron, horrified, shouted abuse and once more set about William with her umbrella. The other ladies looked as if they'd like to see a bit more kissing. The guard found and blew his whistle, and everyone, deafened, froze for a moment.

It took almost ten minutes for Dottie to reassure everyone that she was not being molested. Then it took almost as long again for William to apologise to the guard for misusing his powers as a police officer, calling on the man's human feelings with regard to romance, as it was quite clear by now that Dottie was not in the least a felon on the run. If she was 'of interest' to the police, it was from a purely personal perspective.

The guard's pride was ruffled, and the matron, transferring her disgust to Dottie, had clearly set her down in her mind as 'no better than she should be'. This nonsensical phrase was one often used by her mother's generation to indicate a young woman overly free with her favours, and Dottie was not in the least put out by it.

Eventually they settled back in the compartment. William had hoped to find an unoccupied one, but the train had filled up. He reflected perhaps it was just as well. He was all too ready to get completely carried away by his passionate feelings, and was afraid he might embarrass Dottie with inappropriate behaviour.

Instead it was easier to talk about the events in Lower Bar, in soft voices so as not to wake the older woman again.

William told her about the private enquiry agent who had come forward in London. He enjoyed the way her eyes fixed on him, as she seemed to hang on every word he said.

'So if I can only prove it was someone else who killed Howard Denholme, my brother will be free of the worry of being a wanted man.'

'Well I think I know who it was,' she said. He stared at her.

'His wife,' he said.

She shook her head.

He had another guess. 'The procurator himself? Surely he wouldn't take such a huge risk. But it seems that he'd been having an affair with Mrs Denholme, so perhaps he lost his head and just...'

Dottie shook her head again. 'It was Millicent Masters.'

'What? Who on earth is Millicent Masters?'

'Well, first and foremost, she is the writer of some rather gruesome gangster crime novels.'

He nodded, but she could tell he was still none the wiser.

'And,' she added, feeling that this was her pièce-de-résistance, 'she is the mother of Mrs Denholme.'

He sat back, smiling and shaking his head. 'How do you know this?'

'She told me, in part. And in part I gathered it by gossiping with people. You're not the only detective around, you know.'

'I still don't...'

'Well, it's easy. Mr Denholme forbade his wife to have anything to do with her, and so Mrs Masters couldn't go to the house. She was staying at the inn, at the same time as us.'

'What, that rather large old woman?'

'The one with the beastly little dog, yes. And even her dog's related to the Denholmes' dog. Her dog is Madame Bovary, and theirs is Gustave. Well, the book Madame Bovary was written by Gustave Flaubert, wasn't it, and it's Miss Masters' favourite book. How many Pekineses with French names are there in Lower Bar, do you think? In fact I saw the children running about with their dog and hers, when I went up to the house the second time. And, I saw luggage stacked up inside the back door of the Denholme house, so she's clearly moved in now Mr Denholme is dead. It seems things had come to a head recently when Mr Denholme decided to send one of their sons away to boarding school. He was a brute to his wife, as bad as Billy McHugh; it was not a happy marriage, from what I've heard. On the night I arrived, the night of Denholme's death, I saw Miss Masters walking off along the road with the dog, in the direction of the Denholmes' house.'

'How tall is she?' he asked.

'Not very, I don't think.' Dottie wrinkled her nose, trying to remember if she had ever seen Miss Masters on her feet. 'Why?'

'Well the person who shot Howard Denholme was short.'

'How do you know that?'

'From the position of the wound. Do you think she would be capable of doing such a thing?'

'Oh yes,' Dottie said unhesitatingly. 'I should think she's pretty ruthless if she has to be. She's got a jolly strong handshake too, if that helps. And lots of people in her books get shot, so she probably knows all about firearms. I bet the Denholmes' staff helped with setting the scene afterwards.'

William thought for a few minutes. Then he said, 'I'm still not certain who was behind the thefts and the threatening notes, though I suspect it was Mrs Denholme. The same probably goes for the mysterious fire in the sitting room.'

'They owed money to everyone,' Dottie said. 'The woman in the needlework shop told me that. Perhaps the fire was insurance fraud?'

'Hmm, quite likely. Well, thank you, I think that might bear looking into. I'll be back to work tomorrow.'

'So soon?'

'A policeman's lot is not a happy one,' he said with a grin. He hugged her close, and dropped another kiss on her cheek. 'So, what else did your detective skills find out?'

'Well, let me think. Alex Nelson was the one who did the poaching that they arrested Will for when Anna had to give him an alibi. That was the venison that was in the 'chicken' casserole they served for dinner the last two nights in a row.'

'Hmm come to think of it, Mr Nelson did suggest to me that if anyone should ask, it would be helpful if I could remember the casserole was chicken. I had my suspicions then.'

'Big Billy McHugh is a wife-beater, but that's not exactly a surprise, but you may not know that he is the brother of Mr Nelson's wife.'

'Ah yes. Well I've done some detecting too, you know. Howard Denholme made his money with boot polish.'

She turned and laughed. 'Oh William, everyone knows that.' After a moment she said, 'What time was the crime committed?'

'About eleven o'clock to midnight.'

'Hmm. And it was reported when?'

'Well, the call came through to Forbes at about five minutes to seven the following morning. The maid found him about half an hour earlier.'

'I'm a bit surprised Mrs Denholme was up early enough to know her husband was dead before you did. Did they find him dead, then wake her and tell her immediately?'

William looked puzzled. 'She told me later that she had heard them. She was a bit vague about it. But when I got there fifteen minutes after the call, she had already been sedated by the doctor. Not that I saw him either.'

'That seems awfully quick. Oh but, William, wait! The woman from the needlecraft shop heard the doctor talking to the minister on his way back from the house—at six o'clock. But surely they hadn't even found the dead man by that time?'

William couldn't help a groan of dismay. 'Of course! I bet she was sedated by the doctor long before they rang the police. They wouldn't want to risk me asking her questions, as she appears to be a rather nervy little thing. I bet she was sedated by the doctor just before six o'clock, to make sure she was well and truly under by the time I got there. I know it's been turned over to the Edinburgh fellow, but I want to help Will if I possibly can, it seems the procurator is determined to put this all on him. First thing tomorrow, I'll phone Constable Forbes and tell him to speak to the doctor, then he will need to contact the exchange and see what time the call was put through to the doctor. And the wet mud on the dead man's boots would seem to bear out the idea that everything was staged. They wanted to make it look as though someone came in from outside. In any case, I find it impossible to believe that no one heard the shots. Both barrels? In the dead of night? Even three floors up, the staff—and Mrs Denholme—had to have heard it. they were all in on it, the staff, the wife and this mother with the dog.'

The train wound its way on. They ate tasteless sandwiches and drank revolting railway coffee. Dottie's head presently nodded onto William's shoulder, and soon he himself drifted off to sleep.

They were awoken by a new guard coming through the train, announcing their imminent arrival in York.

'Good,' said the matron, 'That's my stop.' She gave the lovers a look that told them all too clearly that she couldn't wait to be away from their immoral company.

'Change at York for all stations to Scarborough,' the guard said and moved on.

'Scarborough,' Dottie commented. 'George's sister Diana is staying there for a while. She's been ill.' Dottie stretched and yawned.

'I'm not sure we should still consider pregnancy an illness in this day and age,' William said. It was a comment that was to ruin his happiness. How often in the coming weeks and months he wished he had kept his mouth shut.

She turned to look at him. He knew immediately he'd said something he shouldn't have. After all, he was only in Diana's confidence because of the police investigation in which her lover had been murdered. But William had been fast asleep just moments earlier, dreaming of his wonderful future life with his beloved Dottie, and was still gathering his faculties.

'What did you say?' she asked in a colourless voice. 'Pregnant? I'm talking about George's sister, Diana.'

Then she remembered the talk at the dinner table with George's friends, Charles and Alistair, that they had told her about Diana's affair with Archie Dunne.

'George's sister? William? You're saying George's sister, Diana, is pregnant?' she reiterated.

Charles and Alistair had told her about a lot of talk amongst their friends at their club about the dead man, Archie Dunne, and George's younger sister, Diana Gascoigne. She remembered stories she'd heard: of girls 'in trouble' being sent away to have their babies secretly to avoid disgrace to their families and the ruin of their reputation. She thought of Mrs Carmichael, dead, without seeing the man who had once been the baby she had given up for adoption thirty years earlier. Mrs Carmichael who had lived alone for many years, ignored by her former lover and with no news of her only—lost—child.

Dottie's eyes clouded and filled with tears as she realised that her William had kept this secret from her. He had known all along, but had said nothing. Diana had been sent away in secret and disgrace, and they, Flora, George and Dottie, had been told a lie that they had believed. Diana had not had the flu or bronchitis or pneumonia. She had simply got into trouble, and with no man to stand by her and make an honest woman of her, she had been sent away.

And William had known it all. Had always known. He hadn't confided in her, but he had kept the secret imposed on Diana by her parents, colluding with them in Diana's punishment. What else would he keep from her if he kept this back? She felt a conviction now, that he would always keep secrets from her because of his job. He would never be open and honest with her. There would be a part of him she would never know or see. There would be secrets. Things he knew but didn't say. She had foolishly hoped that Diana would recover from her illness. But now that she knew the secret Mrs Carmichael had lived with for thirty years, how could Diana ever truly recover from the same sorrow? Dottie's heart felt as if it crumbled into dust.

Still he hadn't spoken. In those few tiny seconds she had been thinking these thoughts, he hadn't said a word. And now he was looking at her, his face full of his guilty knowledge and self-justification. He had no idea what this meant to her. She felt as though the dusty ruins of her heart blew away on a cold harsh wind.

She didn't know what to say. She hardly knew what she was doing. She stumbled to her feet. The train was slowing down. Dottie cast about her, unsure what to do or say.

William put out his hand. It had all gone wrong, somehow. Softly he said, 'Dottie, darling, I shouldn't have said anything. I'm half asleep, I forgot for a moment it was to be kept quiet...' He put out a hand to her, but she moved away so that he couldn't reach her. The matron was still there, gathering her luggage and watching them closely.

'Dottie, darling,' he pleaded again, more insistently.

'Don't call me that. Tell me what you know.' Her voice was quiet, but not soft as it had been just a short while earlier. No longer the voice of his lover.

He knew it was already too late. There was nothing, nothing, he could say or do now.

'Look, it's because of the investigation into Archie Dunne's murder. Diana was Archie's mistress.'

'I know that.' Her face was white with dismay. She said nothing, and the train slowed even more. He was running out of time.

'She told me when I interviewed her that she was expecting a baby.' They ignored the matron's huff of disapproval. 'Archie's obviously. I—I'm afraid I didn't think... I—I assumed the family would know.'

'We didn't.' She looked about her. The train was very slow now, they would be coming into the station within a minute. 'At least, her parents probably did. I thought her father's behaviour was a bit odd. They said it was pneumonia. They said she was staying with an old nanny whilst she recovered.'

'I imagine they wanted to keep it quiet, for Diana's sake. So she could avoid the shame of it.'

'More likely to avoid their own reputations being sullied.' He was surprised at the bitterness in her tone. Dottie continued, 'But is she all right?'

He shrugged. It was the worst thing he could have done. 'I don't know. I imagine so. I'm not in contact with her. I have her address in my office, but I don't know it offhand. I thought she was at a boarding house. She said nothing about an old nanny.'

The station buildings came into view. The train slowed to a stop. The matron got up to leave, her suitcase, two smaller bags and a bundle tied up in brown paper under her arm, with one last glare at the couple, she pushed past them, banging William's knees with the suitcase.

Dottie was pondering. She looked out at the station. And came to a decision.

'I'm getting off. Help me with my suitcase, please.

I shall be at the Station Hotel in Scarborough. Please let me have the address for Diana as soon as you get back to London. You can leave me a message at the reception desk.'

'Dottie, wait! Sweetheart, think about this a moment! Please don't just...'

'My suitcase, please.'

He got the case down for her, and as she hurried out of the compartment and into the corridor, heading towards the door to the platform. He followed her, pleading with her to see sense.

'Darling! Please, no, Dottie! Think about it. She doesn't want anyone to know. She wants it kept a secret to avoid any scandal to her and her family. Darling, wait!'

She turned fast to hiss through gritted teeth. 'Don't you dare call me Darling, Inspector Hardy!'

She snatched her case from him, stepped lightly down from the train and hurried away through the throng of people. A whistle blew, the train began to pull away, and there was nothing he could do but watch her bright head leaving him behind.

'Dottie!' He hesitated. Should he get down from the train too? But he had to be back at work the next morning. Damn work, he thought, but in any case it was already too late, the train was out of the station, gathering speed. It was too late.

Tears threatened to overwhelm him, and he punched the wall to relieve his distress. He could still see her, at the barrier now, handing in her ticket. She didn't once look back at him.

Almost before it was started, his engagement to Dottie Manderson was over.

William stood there looking out for a few minutes. The station was long gone, the train was racing now through the countryside. He felt frozen, not sure of what to do. The scene replayed itself over and over in his head, pausing now and then like a cinematic film to show him the moments when he had done or said the wrong thing, the moments when the situation could have been salvaged. But it couldn't, he couldn't. It was all too late.

He went to find a seat. Now that he no longer cared, he had the compartment to himself.

THE END

About The Author

Caron Allan writes cosy murder mysteries, both contemporary and also set in the 1920s and 1930s. Caron lives in Derby, England with her husband and two grown-up children and an endlessly varying quantity of cats and sparrows.

Caron Allan can be found on these social media channels and would love to hear from you:

Instagram: caronsbooks

Twitter: caron_allan

Also, if you're interested in news, snippets, Caron's weird quirky take on life or just want some sneak previews, please sign up to Caron's blog! The web address is shown below:

Blog: http://caronallanfiction.com/

Also by Caron Allan:

Criss Cross – book 1 of the Friendship Can Be Murder trilogy

Cross Check – book 2 of the Friendship Can Be Murder trilogy

Check Mate – book 3 of the Friendship Can Be Murder trilogy

Night and Day: Dottie Manderson mysteries book 1

The Mantle of God: Dottie Manderson mysteries book 2

Scotch Mist: Dottie Manderson mysteries book 3: a novella

The Last Perfect Summer of Richard Dawlish: Dottie Manderson mysteries book 4

The Thief of St Martins: Dottie Manderson mysteries book 5

Easy Living: a story about life after death, after death, after death

Coming Soon

The Spy Within: Dottie Manderson mysteries book 6

Made in the USA
Las Vegas, NV
10 February 2022

43684831R00085